MW00629201

Language Of The Heart

Elizabeth Cadell

The Friendly Air Publishing

thefriendlyairpublishing.com

Chapter One

The sun, slanting in through Venetian blinds, shone across Edmund Forth's desk and made a zebra pattern on his secretary's broad back. Seated in his swivel chair, he watched her absently as she sorted all the papers in sight and swept them into a file cradled protectively on her arm.

"That's all, Mr. Forth."

"Thank you, Miss Brady."

"There's nothing else you need see to." Her voice was flat and sensible, like the heels of her neat black shoes. "Mr. Ross has the Peel House drawings, and Mr. Sefton is meeting the York builders tomorrow. Can I have the office keys?"

He handed them over and his glance went from the large, beautifully-furnished room to the City chimneys outside.

"Nice weather for you," Miss Brady commented. "I always think September's the best holiday month."

"Perhaps. Where's the key of—?"

"Your private safe?" She detached a key and gave it to him; then she cleared paperweights, pens and inkstands into drawers—as though, he thought, he were dead and she was

5

clearing away his effects.

"Did Mr. Sefton—" he began.

"—fix that conversion price? Yes. He says the details can wait until you come back."

"Is my..."

"Your pen's here. I filled it."

Neither his father in his time nor he in his, Edmund reflected, had ever had to finish a query about any office matter if Miss Brady was within hearing. He did a swift mental calculation, the answer to which told him that it was thirty-two years since she had come to work for the firm of Forth and Son— first as his father's, then as his own secretary. Once, shortly after joining the firm, he had asked his father how old she was, and his father had been obliged to send for the Appointments File before he could tell him. Then they had learned that she was forty-six, that her name was, unexpectedly, Georgina and that this had been her first London post, as it probably would be her last. That had been—how many?—twelve years ago. Twelve added to forty-six made her fifty-eight. And made him thirty-six. Time was undoubtedly marching on.

"I'll wire you if anything out-of-the-way turns up," she said. "But there'll be nothing else to worry about."

There was nothing to do but go—and as she had said, there would be nothing for him to worry about. He would be away for about three weeks, and in his absence the office, and his home in Chelsea, would run with their usual smoothness and efficiency. On his return, he would merely have to pick up the threads—or the reins—and slip back into his accustomed routine. Sound planning, sound results, his father would have said.

He became aware that Miss Brady was waiting for him to come out of his reverie. She handed him his hat, his rolled umbrella and his brief-case; these in hand, he walked to the door she held open for him, pausing for a moment on the threshold of the main office to prepare himself for a ceremony which, even after nine years, he still regarded as an ordeal: the staff-assembling-to-say-goodbye-to-the-boss.

He passed down the double line of juniors with outward composure; he had no idea what they were thinking, but Miss Brady, following on his heels, could have told him: the boys were noting his impeccable grooming and the girls were gazing with admiration at his tall, strong figure and handsome face, which the horn-rimmed spectacles seemed to make even more grave, more dignified, more distinguished. He had a good deal more presence than his father had ever had, Miss Brady reflected, but he lacked his father's ability to relax at the right moment—like this moment.

He had passed into the corridor and on to Mr. Ross's room, where the senior staff awaited him. Here there was an appearance of ease and informality, with brief discussions as to the route he was taking to Portugal and the cruising speed of his car. Then handshakes, and he was on his way to the lift, Miss Brady on one side of him, and on the other, old Mr. Sefton, who as his godfather, as well as being the oldest member of the firm, was privileged to see him off the premises.

"Miss Wilde telephoned, Mr. Forth," said Miss Brady, her finger on the lift button. "Will you please lunch with her at the house instead of meeting her at the Welton as arranged."

He nodded, overcoming a brief moment of irritation; if he had known that Angela was going to change their plans, he would have used his own instead of the office car.

"Well, goodbye, Edmund," Mr. Sefton said. "Try not to get into any trouble."

His tone was bland, but his eyes held the half-mocking, half-challenging look that lit them whenever he talked to his godson. Edmund ignored the challenge, said goodbye and was borne downwards and out of sight.

"I always," said Mr. Sefton thoughtfully, strolling back to the office with Miss Brady, "succeed in rubbing him up the wrong way."

"You always try hard enough," was Miss Brady's comment. "Why can't you leave him alone?"

"Because he's beginning to get a little, just a leetle bit smug. Haven't you noticed? Well, of course you have, but of course you won't say so."

"He's like his father, and his father was a fine man."

"There's no harm in his being like his father," said Mr. Sefton. "All I'm objecting to is the fact that at thirty-six, he's turning into the rather pompous old boy his father was when he died at the age of sixty-six. All the Forths have a touch of pompousness, or would you call it pomposity, in their make-up, but in our Edmund, it's coming out too soon and too strong. You can see it in his walk." Mr. Sefton, in four paces, succeeded in conjuring up a picture of his godson's rather too rigid bearing. "Dammit, he's letting the blood freeze in his veins. And *she,*" he added, "won't delay the process. Hard as a bag of nuts, and you know it."

"If you're talking about Miss Wilde, I—"

"—regret I cannot comment," finished Mr. Sefton in a perfect imitation of her voice and manner. "Quite, quite, quite. You're a nice, loyal girl—but then, you're not his godfather and so you don't have to worry."

"You don't have to worry either. It's just that he's had a lot of responsibility and—"

"Tosh and tripe, my dear old Brady. He took over a flourishing business and he's had nothing to do but sit back and watch you—and me—running it."

"What about those three prizes he won with his designs in—"

"Oh, I *grant* you he's a better architect than his father ever was—but if he marries that ice block, he's a goner. Can't make out why he wants to."

Miss Brady, who couldn't make out either, decided to wait long enough to discover what else Mr. Sefton had to say on the subject. She disliked his sardonic and too-frank comments, but she respected his nose for news and views.

"She's got looks," she pointed out.

"If you like snow maidens, and if she's a maiden, which is open to doubt. If you want my opinion, he's merely putting her on top of the cake—as decoration. Rich cake, when you consider: large income, good firm, nice little house with servants, impressive car. To say nothing of that property out in Portugal. When you top it all up with a titled blonde, can you blame him for being a bit too pleased with himself ? He...Hey, where're you off to?"

"I work for him, and the office doesn't stop when he goes away." She shepherded the reluctant Mr. Sefton towards his room. "You may be his godfather, but he pays you a salary. Go and earn it."

Mr. Sefton went back to his desk and sat brooding over Edmund. Edmund, in the office car on his way to Lowndes Square, leaned back and in the comfortable, unbroken silence let his mind roam over his affairs—the process his father had called wheel-tapping: a testing, a check-up during which he passed over all that was well and paused to deliberate upon anything that seemed to be interfering with the smooth-running machinery of life.

There didn't, he mused, seem much amiss on either the business or the domestic side. The only thing he would have liked to change was the fact that he was going out to Portugal alone. He had wanted to delay his journey and make it a honeymoon trip, but Angela had rejected the idea out of hand. Incredible though he found it, she disliked Montebarca. She had been driving through Portugal with friends in the Spring and she had made a detour in order to look at the place of which he spoke so often and with such deep affection—and had found nothing, she said, but a cluster of primitive little white houses sitting in the middle of a cork forest. He could, she added, have the place—all to himself.

The estate had been left to him by a distant cousin named Walter Forth, who had stayed briefly at the house in Chelsea when Edmund was about twelve, and had taken a fancy to him, unexpressed at the time but apparent in his Will, in which he left him Montebarca, an estate in the province of Alentejo in Portugal. Edmund, at that time twenty-six, had known little of Portugal. He drove out alone to view the property—and fell unexpectedly, bewilderingly, passionately in love; not with a woman, but with a land, and in particular with the piece of it that he owned. He had gone out every year since; for the first year or so he had taken friends with him, but living conditions were primitive, and he had never found anyone who shared his enthusiasm for the place. He had decided at last that he would ask no more guests until he found a wife who would love the estate as much as he did.

He had found the wife—but once more, he was going out alone.

The car drew up before Lady Wilde's neat, narrow house and the chauffeur came round to open Edmund's door.

"Goodbye, sir. I hope you have a nice trip."

"Thank you, Saunders. You're off with your family to Wales, I hear. I hope you all have a good time."

The last of the office goodbyes; now he could give his mind to his holiday.

A maid admitted him; Miss Wilde was upstairs in the drawing-room, she told Edmund. But as he mounted the stairs, he looked up to see Angela waiting for him at the top, leaning over the delicately-wrought, white-painted balustrade.

"You're punctual; good," she said. "I could only manage two hours, but I thought it would be nicer to lunch here. Mother's out."

He went up the last few stairs and took her in his arms and kissed her. He was not, in spite of his height, very much taller than she was. He looked down at her long, thin, well-boned face, so like her mother's that sometimes—he did not care for Lady Wilde—he experienced a moment of disquiet. She had the same startlingly blue eyes—but they were not china-hard, like her mother's. She had the same beautifully-shaped mouth, but without the malevolent twist. Likenesses, he reassured himself, were as often as not merely surface ones —and Angela possessed attributes notably lacking in her mother: a keen brain, sound common sense and a good head for business. She had managed her own affairs since she was in her teens; now, at twenty-seven, she held an important position on a newspaper and earned a salary that most men would have envied. She had continued to live with her mother, but there was little sympathy between the two, and she had no respect whatsoever for her mother's opinions. Of her father she never spoke; he had drifted away at some time during her childhood and had lately died, unregretted by wife or daughter, at his villa in Nassau.

Her slender body rested lightly against Edmund's for a few moments, and then she freed herself and led him into the drawing room.

"Pour yourself out a drink—and me," she said.

"What made you change your mind and lunch here?"

"They put off the meeting, so I told them I'd take an extra half-hour. I knew Mother was lunching out; I thought we'd have time for a nice talk before you went off to count your corks."

He gave her a drink and sat beside her on the sofa.

"I wish you were coming with me," he said.

"Oh? And what would I do there?"

"There's the vine harvest."

"I've seen several. What else?"

"You could ride."

"On those mares? I thought they were all pregnant, busy having little mules."

"Not all the time."

"What else?"

"Peace and quiet."

"Darling, that sounds wonderful—but I loathe peace and quiet. I think I'll stay at home, thank you very much. When you put in decent sanitation, or even running water, I might go out on a visit.—Why *don't* you?"

"Bring the place up to date? I don't want to. I want to keep it just as it is."

"But it's all so...so *Biblical!* I don't mind looking at Bible pictures, but I don't exactly want to live one! All those women with pots on their heads, and teams of oxen, and mules working the wells and pulling the ploughs.... If you really enjoy it, I've nothing to say, but I do feel it could all do with a few mod cons. No? Well, have it your own way. And now I want to talk about the flat."

He smiled.

"Is that why you needed two hours for lunch?"

"Not especially. Seeing you is always nice—but I did think that if you came here, I'd be able to show you some of the things I'd collected."

She had collected, he saw with surprise on following her into a spare room, more than he would have believed possible. There were vast rolls of material for curtains and chair-covers, lamp shades, pictures, ornaments and all kinds of kitchen equipment.

"One would think," he said, "that we were going to live in it."

"Decorating's fun," she said. "Especially when one's spending somebody else's money. Are you getting alarmed? Do you want to put a limit on the amount?"

He hesitated.

"If we're never going to live there..."

"But our guests are going to."

"Oh?" He sounded amused. "When did you decide that?"

"When you first told me you were going to turn the basement of your house into a garden flat. I was sure you'd never like strangers living there; even if it's self-contained, it's still your house. You'd hear them; you'd see them. What's more, tenants would always be running up to ask you for this or that, or complaining about something. It isn't as though you needed the rent."

"One can always use money." He leaned back and spoke thoughtfully. "We did a good job on that conversion. Odd, isn't it, that my father never thought of doing it? That basement's been useless ever since the kitchen and the servants' rooms were moved upstairs. Now it's a nice, airy little flat. It worked out well."

"It's beautiful. If I weren't going to settle upstairs with you, I'd settle down there on my own. But the guest idea is a good one—or don't you think so?"

"You think they'll like being shown downstairs when they arrive?"

"Why not? They've got a kitchen to make their own breakfasts, and then they can come up to us for the rest of the day. After having made their beds. That way, we shan't have our servants walking out every time guests walk in. Nobody's better at getting or keeping servants than Mother, but even she

15

can't have a free hand about having people to stay— and I like having people to stay."

"You can try it out. Myself, I'd rather not be pushed down into a separate flat when I visited somebody."

"Do you like all the things I've chosen?"

"They look all right."

"All *right!*"

"Well, they're splendid, then."

"Thank you. For that, you can have lunch."

It was not until lunch was over and she was standing in the hall with him, awaiting his taxi, that he remembered a matter he had meant to talk over with her.

"I got a letter from Uncle Robert," he said.

"Oh—him!"

Her voice was edged with contempt, and he laughed. "Him. He's not as bad as that, is he?"

"He's ridiculous. Always calling those family committee meetings. What makes him think he's the head of your family?"

"He **is** the head of the family. He's useful, you know, even if it's only because he saves one a lot of correspondence keeping in touch with distant relations."

"What did he want?"

"Accommodation for two or three weeks."

"For himself?"

"No. For the cousins—Louisa and Frederica."

He saw the angry narrowing of her eyes, and was prepared for her protesting: "You? Oh no! Why you?"

"Because he's run through the rest of the family, I suppose."

"You mean that just because everybody's sick and tired of them and won't have them any more—for which nobody can blame them—you've got to be stuck with two old madwomen?"

"They're not mad, as far as I know."

"They're a nuisance, anyway. Your uncle shouldn't have interfered in the first place; he should have let them work out their own affairs."

"Perhaps. But something's got to be done with them."

"You're a bachelor—you can't have two old women fastened on to you. Especially two old eccentrics you've never set eyes on, cousins or not. Write and tell your uncle that you're going away and you've no idea when you'll be back. No, don't. Tell him quite clearly, once and for all, that they're his problem and not yours. Why didn't you write in the office this morning?"

"I wanted to discuss it with you."

"Well, you've discussed it. Write and tell him that the only possible solution is to find a home and put them in it."

"Surely an institution of that kind isn't—"

"Who said anything about an institution?" she asked irri-

17

tably. "I simply mean a nice, comfortable house for old people, where they'll be quite happy with a room of their own and lots of other old people to talk to. They'll be well looked after and they'll settle down perfectly well."

"Yes, but—"

"Which would *you* rather do if you were in their place? Be pushed from place to place, planted on people who don't in the least want you—or settle down permanently in some nice quiet country house?"

"It isn't exactly—"

"How long is it since those two came home from India?"

"About four years, as far as I can remember."

"Four years—and since then, all they've done is cadge."

"I wouldn't call it cadging. They simply—"

"—cadge. Write to your Uncle Robert and tell him what I've said and let him work out his own problems.—Here's your taxi."

He lingered for a moment after saying goodbye.

"Can't I give you a lift?"

"No, thanks. Somebody's picking me up."

They had been engaged for two months, they were to be married in two more, but she still used a detached, impersonal tone when referring to her friends. If he pressed for names, she merely pointed out that if it was somebody he had met, the name would mean something; if not, there was no point in being specific. He was left on these occasions with a feeling half pique, half annoyance—but he had learned that it was better to drop the subject before it developed into a quarrel. He was also learning that her calm, cold, rather drawling voice gave to everything she said an authority that he sometimes mistook for wisdom; it was not until he was away from her, from her blonde beauty, her elegance, her clear, decisive pronouncements, that he began to have doubts as to the soundness of her judgment.

The taxi bore him homeward; his car was waiting for him outside his house. Before going indoors, he went down the steps to the new flat and walked round the empty rooms. They had been cleared of the last sign of workmen; the floors were scrubbed and the windows clean; the stove and the refrigerator were in place. Angela could start furnishing, knowing her ability to get the utmost out of every firm she dealt with, he had no doubt that on his return she would have the flat almost ready for occupation.

He walked up to street level and went into his own part of the house. In the hall were his packed suitcases; Mr. and Mrs Yates, the married couple who looked after him, were waiting, like the office staff, to go through the ceremony of leave-taking. He had only to change into more comfortable clothes, write a cheque for expenses during his absence and drive away.

A short time later, he was seated at the wheel of his car. His suitcases were behind.

Ahead was Montebarca.

Chapter Two

The journey was as pleasant as he always found it; his car was fast and comfortable and after a process of trial and error, he had chosen the route he liked best, and now seldom diverged from it: Tours, St. Jean Pied-de-Port, Roncesvalles, Burgos, Guarda, Coimbra and so to Lisbon. At Lisbon, he spent a day with the lawyers who in his absence were in charge of the finances of Montebarca—and then he had crossed the Tagus and was driving towards the Alentejo.

He had never before come out so late in September, never seen the land so burnt and dry. The heat, considerable in Lisbon, became intense; he stopped to change into a cooler shirt, and he put on to the car seat a straw cover which he had bought at Setubal and which lifted him an inch or so off the hot leather upholstery. When he drove past points at which road repairs were in progress, dust rose in heavy clouds from the untarred surfaces and filled the car. He passed miles of parched stubble; in places where it had been set alight, the flames seemed to him to leap and bound like frightened animals striving to out-distance the car.

Past Vendas Novas, he was in cork country. He looked

out at the familiar trees, not tall, but giving an impression of height by reason of being set far apart, and standing clear of scrub. The country here was more broken; olive groves alternated with bare, boulder-strewn tracts. He did not find it difficult to understand why this was considered one of the least picturesque provinces of Portugal—but for him, its olive and ilex and cork trees, its groves of eucalyptus, the reddish-brown of its parched acres, had a beauty of their own. The district had a wildness, a spaciousness, a sombreness he had grown to love.

Past Montemor, and on to Arraiolos. He picked out a shady patch of woodland, stopped the car and got out to eat a picnic lunch, and doe-eyed children seemed to materialise from the undergrowth and settled down with complete unselfconsciousness to watch him. In the early days, he remembered, he had rather bungled this kind of thing—but now he knew the form: a smile, a word of greeting, politely uttered and as politely returned, and an invitation to join him. Grapes? No thank you; they had their own grapes growing in profusion. Figs? Figs, too, they had, and bread, and wine but if the Senhor wasn't going to eat all that succulent sausage, or that cold pie, or that cold fish dish...

It was all very companionable, and he was almost reluctant to leave—but at the end of the journey was Montebarca.

He drove on at last, fast and without pause, past Estremoz, with its pinnacle of white buildings set on the hillside; on to Elvas, long since familiar to him as his nearest market town, his post and telegraph office and his last link with civilisation.

He did not enter the town; his way lay beyond it, but not in the direction of Spain. Here he was to leave main roads and take one that began as a straggling line on the map and trailed away to nothing. Metalled surfaces gave way to dusty roads; dusty roads lost themselves in stony, rutted tracks. He was in low gear, keeping an eye open for the worst potholes; the sun beat down mercilessly and the car was an oven—but for all the discomfort, he felt a sense of well-being flooding him. Everything was as right as possible; there was not a hitch anywhere. Far be it from him to take undue credit for what perhaps was only luck—but all the same, he couldn't help feeling that good planning had something to do with it.

It was precisely at this point in his musings that he rounded a bend in the road and came upon the breakdown.

He had time, as he approached, to note that the car was a large, black, outdated model. It was also mud-streaked, deeply scratched and had dents where rounded surfaces should have been. It stood at the side of the road, its engine open to view; viewing it dejectedly were three people: a white-haired, sturdy-looking man in his sixties, a boy of about twelve and a girl a little younger. Round them were grouped a few peasants waiting for something to happen.

As he brought his car to a stop, the girl gave a cry of delight.

"Gosh! Look—a *car!*" She rushed across the road to address Edmund through the window. "Donkey carts, mule carts,

22

donkeys without carts and mules without carts—but no cars," she explained. "We...I say, you speak English, don't you?"

"It's an English number-plate, idiot," the boy called.

Edmund got out and found the elderly man coming across the road to speak to him. Like the children, he looked untidy and travel-stained, but he had great dignity of bearing. His speech was slow, formal and precise.

"It is very kind of you to stop, sir," he said. "We were beginning to fear that no motor traffic used this road. I am sorry that my knowledge of engines is scanty, and so I have not been able to be of any assistance. The vehicle"—he gave a distasteful glance at it and averted his eyes—"has not been giving satisfaction."

He was following Edmund to the black car; on the way, he gave his name as Teck.

"I am in the service of Miss Nash, sir," he said. "These are Miss Belinda Nash and Master Kerry Nash, the sister and brother of Miss Nash. Miss Nash left to try to get the assistance of a trained mechanic."

"She went to Elvas on a donkey," Belinda explained. "First a beastly tramp steamer, then a *pitiful* car, and then a donkey. Myself, I think we'd all better get donkeys and go the rest of the way on them."

Edmund had had a glimpse of the interior of the car, and it did nothing to clarify his ideas on the stranded passengers. The suitcases were expensive leather ones, but they were very old, battered beyond belief and fastened with rope or twine.

"We thought we were here for keeps," Belinda said. "For ever and ever. Nothing but dust and—"

"Oh, get out of the *way*," implored her brother, "and let's get a look at the damage, can't you? It's a wreck, isn't it?" he went on to Edmund, who was bending over the engine. "I *said* it wouldn't do the journey—didn't I, Teck? I *told* her. I don't know much about cars, but I do know that much."

Teck took no part in the discussion; he had placed himself beside Edmund, ready to do what was required of him, but it was the two children who did all the talking—far, far too much, Edmund thought.

"It's an awful car, isn't it, Mr.... did you say your name?" Belinda asked.

"Forth."

"Well, isn't it a terrible car?"

"He can see, can't he?" said Kerry. "Mr. Forth, can you do anything? I mean, do you know anything about car engines?"

Edmund said that he did. He was feeling that he did not, after all, care for children as much as he had imagined. The voices of these two were high and shrill and rang in his right and left ears respectively. They were both rather plain, with freckled, very dirty faces, small upturned noses and brown, bright, beseeching eyes. They wore coloured shirts and blue jeans and grimy tennis shoes. At their hands he preferred not to look.

"We were had, weren't we, Mr. Forth?" Belinda asked him. "I mean, they shouldn't have sold this car to us. They—"

"Can you blame them?" Kerry asked bitterly. "Can you? They told her it needed lots more done to it, and what did she say? She said she was sure it would get us home. I told her—"

"Oh, all *right!*" broke in Belinda irritably. "You've been telling us and telling us all the way from Lisbon. Can you make it go, Mr. Forth?"

Edmund straightened and made his report. He would have liked to make it to Teck, who he felt to be the responsible member of the party, but the two children seemed to be awaiting his reply.

"You're lucky"—he addressed all three—"to have managed to do the journey out from England. The car—"

"*Out?*" Kerry's voice was high with astonishment. "Out? You don't think we drove this thing out from England?" "Out!" Belinda, overcome by helpless mirth, held on to Edmund's jacket for support. "Out!" she gasped. "Oh my goodness, that's jolly funny!"

"You mean"—Edmund made a vain effort to release himself from her grip—"you mean you didn't come out to Portugal in this car?"

"No." Belinda, with an effort, controlled her mirth. "We came out *with* the car."

"We came out, sir," explained Teck, "in a...in a ship, bringing the car with us."

"Ship? You call that a ship?" Belinda shuddered. "It was a tramp steamer, that's all it was. It was terrible! And now we're stuck here. Are we stuck for good, Mr. Forth?"

"I can fix you up for the moment," he said, "but I'm afraid you'll have to stop at a garage in Elvas. It wasn't wise to leave the main road; if you do, you're likely to come across some rough surfaces—like this one."

"It's the distributor lead, isn't it?" Kerry asked, hanging over the engine. "That's what I thought it was, when I looked."

"That's the immediate trouble," said Edmund, "but there are others."

And would be still more, he reflected; the engine, like the suitcases, appeared to be held together by string.

"Well, it's got to get us home," Belinda said. "I'm not going on any more tramp steamers. Fran told us it would be a cargo boat, only smaller, and because it was smaller and there were no other passengers, she said we'd have a lovely time. Lovely time! Ask Teck! Ask him how many times I was sea-sick! It was a wreck—like this car—wasn't it, Teck?"

"It was not, if I may say so, of the luxury class," Teck said cautiously. "You thought it would—"

"I thought it would be lovely and white and shining." She gave a scornful laugh that Sarah Bernhardt could not have bettered. "White and shining? It was rusty inside and outside, and it was falling apart, and it smelt." She held her nose until she turned red in the face, and then released it. "And, Mr.

26

Forth, d'you know what they gave us to eat, every single day? They—"

"He doesn't *care* what you had to eat," Kerry broke in. "Why can't you stop talking about the part of the trip that's over and let's talk about the trip home? Mr. Forth, will we get home? There was a terrible noise in the engine, and I told Fran I thought it was the big end, but—"

"—but she doesn't know a big end from a hole in the road," said Belinda, "so what does she do? She buys a car. Twenty-seven whole pounds gone, just like that." She snapped her lingers, "Twenty-seven pounds—for a wreck. For two wrecks. The tramp steamer was the other one, and she would've bought that too if we hadn't got on free. Just because we got free passages is no reason to feed us on—"

"You were as keen on coming as anybody else was," Kerry reminded her.

Edmund bent over the engine once more, and the children leaned on either side of him, watching with absorption as he worked and giving him for a short while respite from their chatter. At last he straightened.

"Let's try starting her now," he said. "Can you—"

Kerry was scrambling into the driver's seat. After one or two abortive attempts, the engine spluttered into life; there was a putt-putt-putt and then the car began a series of spasmodic jerks that sent Kerry bobbing up and down like a cork. The noise was deafening.

"She went, Mr. Forth!" Kerry said triumphantly, switching off at a signal from Edmund.

"She won't go far," Edmund said. "When your sister gets back, you can tell her that you'll be able to get as far as the garage in Elvas—and if I may advise you, it would be better to take the most direct route home."

"There goes the last balloon," Belinda said bitterly. "We were going to roam—that was the word she used—roam. We were going to roam from Lisbon to the Spanish border, and up through Spain, still roaming, and through France. If we get to Spain, it'll be a miracle, and if we get to France, it'll be at the end of a tow-rope."

"What I'm wondering," Kerry said, scanning the horizon anxiously, "is where Fran's got to. She's been gone two hours."

"And if she got to the garage," pointed out Belinda, "what would she say? All the Portuguese she knows is Wah and How. Can you speak Portuguese, Mr. Forth?"

He said that he could, and then there was a moment's silence during which he acknowledged to himself that it would have been kind to offer to lead them into Elvas and aid them at the garage. But he did not make the offer. He was anxious to get on, and he had had enough of Kerry and Belinda. When Fran, whoever she was, came back on her donkey, they could be on their way; he had made them mobile and he saw no reason for doing more. This was the time he liked to arrive at Montebarca—the hour before dusk, when there was still light enough to stand on his hillside and gaze through the trees at

28

the almost limitless view—to his left, the plains of Spain; to his right, the white buildings of Elvas.

He accepted the offer of the oily rag Teck held out to him, wiped his hands and walked over to his car.

"Well—thanks awfully," said Kerry.

"Thank you, sir." Teck accompanied him to his car and opened the door. "You have been most kind. I am sorry Miss Nash was not here to thank you herself, but she—"

"There she is!" shouted Belinda. "*FRAN!*"

The scream tore across Edmund's nerves; it was followed by a hoarse yell from Kerry.

"Fran! Come on! We can go!"

From the distance came the sound of a whistle—long, clear and piercing. Belinda and Kerry attempted to answer it, but their efforts had nothing of the sweetness and clarity of the one that had come through the still air. Once again came the sound, and Edmund turned and stared down the narrow, dusty road.

At first he could see nothing—and then, following Kerry's gaze, he looked up at the parched grass banks that bordered the road on one side... and stood riveted to the spot on which he stood.

Nothing was visible, in those first moments, but a pair of legs straddling a donkey. The upper half of their owner was hidden behind the light, hanging branches of a tree—but in the brief moments before the rest of the body came into view,

Edmund held his breath, waiting for proof of his conviction that no figure, no face could measure up to the perfection, the matchless beauty of those long, slender, exquisite brown legs, bare save for the light sandals that dangled from the toes.

He waited, motionless and entranced. The whistle came again—and then he saw Fran Nash.

His first feeling was one of satisfaction at the accuracy of his estimate: nothing could measure up to those legs. The figure was good, but the face, he thought, did not merit a second glance.

But he found himself giving it a second glance—and then a third. Sister to the other two; so much was obvious. Brown straight hair, small nose, brown eyes; one of those high-cheekboned faces that came out well in photographs. Nothing outstanding about it—except, perhaps, the eyes. They were not particularly large, but they were set aslant, and they were fringed by lashes so thick that he had to wait until she came close before he could believe that they were real.

He judged her to be little more than twenty. For the rest, he found her appearance as untidy, her manner as free and easy and as casual as that of her brother and sister. Her shirt was a faded blue; her shorts, brief and close-fitting, had once been white. She sat easily, carelessly on the donkey, smiling at Kerry and Belinda as they ran to meet her, coming on without pause, listening to their account of Edmund's arrival and help with the car.

Then she halted beside him and he became aware of the

overalled man walking beside the donkey.

"Mechanic, Portuguese," she said. "It took them an hour to understand that I wasn't touring Portugal on a borrowed donkey, so in the end I drew them a picture of a broken-down car, and they got the idea—but would they send a mechanic with a car? No. They wanted to do it the polite way, so he's been trotting beside me all the way from Elvas." And looking, Edmund noted, as though he had enjoyed the journey. The girl, he thought, had the same conversational technique as her brother and sister—to open the mouth and let it say exactly what it liked, though this girl said it in a rather attractive voice and not on the high C used by the other two.

She had dismounted and was addressing, for the most part in sign language, a wizened old man who had taken the donkey's rein.

"He's the owner," she explained to Edmund. "When he passed by and saw the car wouldn't go, he offered me the donkey—just like that. It's an absolutely heavenly donkey— it practically talks; if I lived out here, I'd buy it, if he'd sell it. What do I have to pay him for two hours' donkey ride?"

There was no need for Edmund to reply, for the owner, with a beaming, toothless smile and a wave of his broad-brimmed felt hat, indicated that the pleasure had been entirely his, and with his donkey, went on his way.

"Well, that was nice," Fran remarked. "I like these Portuguese. Every time we stopped to buy melons when we were thirsty, they presented us with one. At the garage just now they

31

insisted on giving me a cool drink. Will you tell the mechanic you've fixed the car, Mr...."

"Forth. Edmund Forth."

"Sounds like a king," she commented. "Edmund Forth. Edmund the Engineer. Well, thanks awfully for doing it."

"It's only a temporary repair, I'm afraid," he said.

"There's heaps and heaps wrong," Belinda told her. "I told you you shouldn't have paid twenty-seven pounds, Fran."

"You can't get a good car for less," said Fran. "And it carried four people all the way from Lisbon to here. Let's see you doing that when you're as old as that car.—What's the mechanic saying, Mr. Forth?"

"He says he'll need two or three days to put things right," translated Edmund.

"Two or three days! Gosh!" she exclaimed in dismay.

"There's a good Government *pousada* just outside Elvas," Edmund said. "You'll be very comfortable there."

"Is that where you're going?" asked Belinda.

"Me?" The frank question took him off his guard. "No. I'm... I'm going on."

"Have you just come out from England, or are you just going back?" she asked.

"I've just come out."

He spoke more coolly than he intended. He resented the artless questions, but he was also recovering from the shock of almost having asked them to come with him to Montebarca.

The invitation had been on his tongue, and all that had prevented him from giving voice to it had been a sudden vision of them all invading his quiet fastness: the garrulous younger ones, the whistling older one, the old man. Kindly impulses were all very well, but a man coming upon a stranded family didn't have to gather them all under his roof. There was no lack of accommodation nearby; they could be at the *pousada* in less than an hour, and they could amuse themselves in Elvas until their car was ready for the road.

He saw the girl Fran's eyes on him, sober and speculative. They were extraordinarily intelligent eyes, he noted— and almost too easy to read. He saw their expression change from speculation to certainty: she had sensed that he had had a choice to make, and had guessed that he had made it in some way that was less than complimentary to herself and to her companions.

"Well, thanks again," she said. "Belinda, Kerry, Teck— thank the kind genl'um."

Something in the light mockery of her tone made him angry.

"If I may advise you," he said formally, "I think you'd better keep to the main roads in future."

"We'll do that," she promised. A smile irradiated her face. "You wouldn't like to swap what Teck calls vehicles?"

He smiled somewhat frostily, shook his head, got into his car and drove away to the shouts and waves of the two younger ones. Once out of their sight, he settled down in his seat and waited for a wave of relief to engulf him; instead, he felt nothing but irritation and a sense of injury. He had done his best for them, and the girl had looked at him as though she had sized him up and found something amiss. Was it to be expected that he would arrive at Montebarca accompanied by an archaic car, several broken suitcases, two vociferous children, an old attendant—and a girl whose whistle would cause a stampede of all the animals within a radius of miles? Was it? He thought not.

He put them resolutely out of his mind, and turned his attention to guiding the car over the increasingly rough surface. He was leaving civilisation behind; he was journeying from the present into the past; the road was a stony waste, and the car lurched from side to side and threatened to slip into the deep, dried-up ditches and crevices left by last year's floods. A tiny village, and then another—and then no more; the road, now wide and level, with the stones heaped neatly at its edges, began to rise gently round the shoulder of a hill. His hill: he could see affixed to the trees the little wooden boards indicating that this was protected property. His property.

Once, long ago, he had thought of making some kind of boundary; he had felt that an estate should have its extent clearly marked. But he had decided against that, and other, changes. His early zeal to modernise had given way to a desire to keep things exactly as they were, for as long as possible. The day of the tractor was drawing nearer—but it was not here yet. Walter Forth's father had bought Montebarca, and the descendants of his employees were still here, doing everything in the way that their forefathers had done, he wanted no changes. He wanted only to preserve the peace, the productivity of the estate.

To the left were his cork trees, to the right his olive groves, with the little, rounded, evenly-spaced trees that always reminded him of a child's drawing of a forest. He drove over a bridge, beneath which flowed a thin, sluggish stream; he had last seen it in March, when the water was almost up to bridge level, rushing noisily towards the vineyards and past the orchard, which he could see now through the trees—a patch of brilliant green almost startling against the sober tints surrounding it. There were lemons and oranges down there, and magnificent fig trees; there were plums and pears and peaches and nectarines and walnuts and pomegranates. There too were his flowers, growing almost untended: roses and hibiscus, camellia, oleander, brilliant against hedges of yew. There were magnolia trees and borders of lavender....

He drew a deep breath. He was here. There above him, through the trees, were his loved white buildings, bright with bougainvillia, shaded by overhanging vines.

In the brief space between stopping the car and getting out to greet the men, women and children assembled to receive him, he had time to admit to himself that Angela's description of the place might well be applied: a cluster of primitive little houses set in a forest clearing. But as he stepped out and found one of his hands seized and kissed by old Maria-Jesus, and his other warmly shaken by his stocky, handsome bailiff, he forgot everything but the fact that he was at home, in a sense he felt at home nowhere else. He was master here, and though they saw him seldom, he knew that these people were his own in an almost feudal sense, bound to him by ties of loyalty and the reassuring sense of continuity: James Forth, his son Walter— and now another Forth; himself.

He could see, through the long wooden bead curtains that hung in the doorway, the vast windowless Alentejo kitchen, built in the centre of the house; he could see its ceiling of great black rafters, and the wood embers in the fireplace—a fireplace large enough to accommodate half a dozen little wooden chairs on which the cold sat to warm themselves, the hungry to hug a bowl of warm soup.

He was shaking hand after hand, in strict seniority: Tia Maria-Jesus, who had cooked at that fire for nearly sixty years and who was the acknowledged authority on everything from the master's wishes to the herbs necessary to cure every illness on the estate. After her, the bailiff, Domingo, manager of Montebarca and answerable only to Edmund and to the lawyers in Lisbon, to whom he sent weekly accounts. After Domingo, his wife and eight children. Then the foreman, José, who had no wife and no family; after him, the man in charge of the orchard; the head mule-man, the head oxen-man; Bruno, who was in charge of the wine lodge; Manuel, who was in charge of the mares. Handshakes and smiles, questions and answers, pleasure evident on every face. This was home, and this was, as always, a heart-warming welcome home.

One by one, they dispersed, and at last he went indoors—into the cool, stone-floored house, sparsely furnished, every-thing—with one exception—exactly as it had been in the time of Walter Forth. The exception had been the pictures on the walls, which, after a year or two of trial, Edmund had felt un-able to bear any longer. He had taken them down, and Tia Maria-Jesus had taken them away. Next year, when he came, they were on the walls again. He had taken them down and again found them hanging up on his return; the ceremony had continued to the present day.

It was dusk, and the maids—Zefa and Conceição and Laurinda—were lighting the lamps. He ordered a bath, and huge jars of hot water were brought and poured into the round, low, shallow clay bath; Zefa stood ready to pour in the cold water he needed.

Dinner at the vast table—Edmund had been unable to find out why James Forth, who had only one son, needed a din-ing table that seated twelve. Soup with something that looked like chopped grass floating on top; one of his own chickens; hard, brownish bread baked in the bread oven that he could see out of one of the windows; his own grapes, figs and melons; cheese made from sheep's milk; his own wine.

And as always, the deep, almost incredible silence, bro-ken only by the swish-swish of Zefa or Laurinda's heavy skirts as they waited upon him; the murmur of voices in the kitchen, the soft clashing of the wooden beads in the doorways.

And in his bare, white-washed bedroom, lying on the iron bedstead with its mattress of straw, all sounds were stilled, save those of the crickets. He blew out the lamp and lay waiting for the peace to engulf him.

But his last thoughts before sleeping were not, oddly enough, of Montebarca. They were of a girl with a speculative gaze that had weighed him up and—for no reason he could see—found him wanting.

Chapter Three

He was up the next morning at six, and for the next two days was constantly in the company of his bailiff. He inspected the cork that had been cut in July; he walked through the vineyards and agreed that the harvest would be a bad one. He went down to the orchard and up to the newly- planted eucalyptus groves, to the wine lodge and to the olive presses and the brandy distillery—and everywhere he went, his workers, the placid, soft-voiced, even-tempered, kindly and polite *Alentejanos* paused to greet him, or to make their report, or to answer his questions.

He had learned much since his first visit. He had come to Montebarca year after year; sometimes twice a year. He had chosen to come at different seasons, so that he had seen the ploughing and the sowing, the summer drought and the winter floods, the grain harvest and the grape harvest. He had sold pigs at Sousel and bought oxen at Elvas; he had watched the pruning and the cutting-back of old, unproductive trees to provide firewood and charcoal; he had come in the shooting season and shot his own game. There was still much to learn— but each time he went back to England, he felt that he had put down his roots a little farther into Alentejo soil.

Two nights after his arrival, Domingo gave him a message from Elvas: there was sherry for him, if he wanted it.

He decided that he would go in and fetch it. He made a practice of taking sherry back to England with him; sometimes he drove over the border and bought it in Spain, but if he did not feel like going so far, he went into Elvas and made a deal with a *contrabandista.*

He set off after breakfast. It was a cloudy morning; Domingo, seeing him off, prophesied rain, and before he had driven far, a heavy downpour was making his windscreen wipers all but useless. At Elvas, a dozen bottles of sherry were wrapped and carried carefully to the car—and then he was making his way out of the town, on which an uncertain sun was now shining.

He came down a hill with caution, skidding a little as he passed a lorry laden with pink marble. As he swung back to the right side of the road, he glanced ahead and stiffened to attention.

A breakdown.

Swiftly, he took in the details. A skid, probably; the large, too-familiar black car was being hauled by strong hands out of the ditch. Fran Nash, her brother and sister and the old man, Teck, were standing watching the operation.

He approached slowly, but his mind was working fast. They were in trouble again. He had to pass them; if they saw him, he would have to stop—and he did not want to stop. They were not, now, on a by-road; this was the main route from Portugal to Spain and the volume of traffic was heavy. Somebody would stop and help them; this time, it need not be himself. He decided to let the lorry overtake him; in its shelter, he would drive past. They would not see him behind the highly piled marble. He would drive on and be safely on his way back to Montebarca.

His plan worked. The road was clear enough, wide enough to allow him to keep abreast of the lorry; at what he considered a safe distance ahead, he accelerated.

And then, above the lorry's clatter, he heard the piercing, ear-splitting whistle.

He would have given almost anything to have driven on, but something seemed wrong with his co-ordination. His head was counselling speed, but his foot was already on the brake. He found himself in reverse, backing towards the black car; while his mind continued to point out the undesirability of embroiling himself further in the affairs of this girl who whistled, he was drawing nearer and nearer to her.

She walked across the road and waited for him to come to a halt. She looked as calm and as untroubled as she had looked on the donkey.

"For one moment," she said, "I thought you were going past without saying goodbye."

"Hi!" yelled Belinda, skipping across the road in Kerry's wake and missing a van by inches. "Isn't it funny how you always come along when we've broken down?"

"We haven't broken down," Fran said. "All we did was skid. They've just pulled us out of the ditch and we're going on. Gosh, that was rain, wasn't it!"

They were on their way. Greatly relieved, Edmund accompanied them to the black car, and the friendly group of lorry drivers who had lifted it out of the ditch parted to make way for them.

"Be careful of wet roads," said Edmund. "There's a bit on the other side of the border that—"

"Oh, we're not heading for Spain," Fran told him. "We're going home."

He looked at her in surprise.

"But—"

"We're going back. The ship we came out on is still in Lisbon, but she sails tomorrow. When she leaves for home, we'll be on her. Next time I buy a car, it'll be a Rolls-Royce with a chauffeur screwed down at the wheel."

"Can you *imagine*!" Belinda asked in disgust. "When I got off that boat, I thought I'd never see the beastly thing again."

Edmund was looking at Fran. "What made you decide not to—"

"- go and see all those places we thought we'd see? That was a nice idea," she explained, "but I should have paid twenty-eight pounds for a car instead of being mean and sticking at twenty-seven. The garage people said we'd only get this one to

England if we hitched it behind a tractor. They didn't exactly say that, but that was the general idea. So we're catching the boat before it sails tomorrow—we were offered two-way free passages if we wanted them, and we do want them. All I wish is that I hadn't wasted all that time and money getting a driving licence— What's that man saying?"

The man, driver of one of the lorries, had been examining the wheels of the black car, and what he had to say was brief and to the point: the front wheels had not been improved by resting in the ditch, and would have to be adjusted.

"Well, tell him to adjust them," requested Fran. "We're in a hurry. *You* go and see, Mr. Forth, will you please?"

There was silence as Edmund made his examination. At the end of it, he straightened and met Fran Nash's anxious eyes.

"Well?" she asked.

"You can't go on, I'm afraid," he said. "Not until those wheels have been seen to. They—"

"We've got to go on." She spoke decisively. "We've got to catch that boat. If we miss it, we're stuck for two weeks before the next one of the same line can take us back. We've got to get to Lisbon. It's only a matter of hours, after all; what's a crooked wheel or two? Somebody can straighten them out, can't they? I can drive slowly and we can keep going and—"

"You can't even get going," Edmund told her.

His tone was cool. Inexperienced drivers, he was thinking, shouldn't pile their families into a wreck of a car and set off light-heartedly on long trips. They merely came to grief, and somebody had to come to their rescue.

"Look." Fran addressed him slowly and clearly. "I've just said that we've got to get to Lisbon, and I meant it. I don't mind if the car folds up the moment we get it aboard— but I've got to catch that boat."

"It's quite impossible—in that car," he said. "If I thought there was a chance of your doing it, I'd tell you so— but there isn't. You won't be able to drive anywhere with the wheels in that condition. I can take you all back to Elvas in my car and leave you at the *pousada* and—"

"The what?"

"The Government—"

"Oh that! We didn't go there. Our budget, for anybody who's interested, doesn't run to *pousadas,*" she told him.

"Well, if you go back to the place you stayed at—"

"The place we stayed at was a nice comfortable field owned by a nice accommodating farmer. We slept in sleeping bags. We always have slept in sleeping bags: on the boat because there were no cabins for us, and on the trip, or on the bit of the trip we managed to do. Teck slept in the car because he's too old to rough it; that's why I had to have a big car. We don't in the least mind going on sleeping in sleeping bags, but after paying the bill at the garage, where I think they must have put in an entire new engine, all made of gold, our finances don't run to a return journey through Spain and France. So we have to catch that boat—now do you see? If we don't, we'll all be on the parish until the next one comes in."

"If you can't go on, you can't," he said. "It's unfortunate, and I'm sorry, but if you don't mind my saying so, a car like that one wouldn't have got you far without trouble, and twenty-seven pounds was too much to pay for it. Twenty-seven pounds too much. Your best plan is to transfer your luggage to my car and stay with me until your car's put right; then you can go back to Lisbon and catch the boat you mentioned. You can't sleep in sleeping bags after this rain."

It was, he knew, the only thing to be done. He couldn't drive away and leave them stranded. He was aware that his invitation had been less than warm, but he had been unable to inject more cordiality into it.

"You mean"—it was Belinda speaking in the tone of one who saw reprieve at hand—"you mean you've got a *house* here?"

"Yes."

"Gosh! You mean we can *stay* with you?"

"I think that would be the best plan."

He saw Fran's eyes on him.

"You're absolutely certain we can't get that boat?" she asked.

"Yes. I'll send a message by one of these lorry drivers and have your car collected and taken back to Elvas. You and your brother and sister—and Teck—had far better come with me."

She was, he saw, as unwilling to come as he had been to invite them. Her eyes rested on the black car, and for a moment he thought she was going to abandon it and ask him to help them to get to Lisbon. Then she looked at him once more.

"If we really can't go on," she said, "we'd be glad to accept your offer."

She did not sound enthusiastic. She did not even, he noted with resentment, sound particularly grateful. In silence, he helped Teck to load their luggage into his car; then he put Teck and the children behind and took his place at the wheel, with Fran beside him.

"How far?" she enquired.

"We'll be there in about forty minutes."

"D'you live out here?" Kerry asked.

"No. I come out every year."

"Why don't you live in your house always?" Belinda wanted to know.

"Because I have a job in London."

She and Kerry asked, he estimated, eight hundred questions on the way to Montebarca, and his monosyllabic answers did nothing to discourage them. Any normal sister, he thought, would have checked their volubility, but Fran merely sat back comfortably against the cushions, saying nothing. She had a slow, lazy manner that made a strange contrast to her swift, light speech. She seemed to be dormant for a time, and then would rouse herself and deliver a series of sentences so rapid that he had difficulty in following all she said.

They were received at Montebarca with a warmth which Edmund thought excessive. Tia Maria-Jesus kissed hands all round, and after counting the visitors and deciding that Zefa and Conceição and Laurinda needed reinforcements, sent down to the fields for her grand-daughters, Isaura and Josefina. Fran and Belinda were put into the double guest room; Kerry had the single one and Teck was made comfortable in the room known as the grape room, since in it bunches of grapes were hung to dry on strings suspended from wall to wall.

The luggage was carried in, Teck finding himself constantly circumvented when he attempted to do what he considered to be his work. Lunch was carried out to the long wicker table in front of the house; by half past one, Edmund was seated at its head, with Fran at the foot and the children between them; behind his chair, Teck stood with the wine bottle in his hand and a determined expression on his face; nobody was going to wrest from him this task.

It was impossible to remain for long unmoved by the two children's enthusiasm for everything around them. The straw mattresses, the primitive sanitation, the groups of little white houses, the bread oven, the vast water barrels—all these kept their tongues wagging throughout the meal. Only at the end was there silence—the silence of satiation.

Edmund made only one rule: they were to wear wide-brimmed straw hats. The sun, here, was not a friend but an enemy, and sunstroke was not a joke but a probability.

They sat at a table under the grape-vine canopy. Nearby sounded the plop-plop of clothes banged on stone; a young girl named Ana was bent over a shallow, circular bowl which was balanced on a plank set across two boulders; the shadow of the great, scarlet water barrel fell across her, and round it, hens pecked, turkeys gobbled and peacocks spread their gaudy tails. An oxen cart creaked its way up the track from the well, bringing a full barrel of water with which to replenish the scarlet one. A little way away, Zefa and two small boys dragged bunches of brushwood towards the bread oven; black smoke poured from its chimney and an old woman in black, the inevitable scarf and wide-brimmed straw hat on her head, bent to improvise a little broom of eucalyptus leaves with which to sweep aside the embers when the oven was hot. A mule-drawn cart clattered up from the orchard, piled high with fruit and vegetables; when it went back for a further load, Belinda and Kerry were perched behind the driver. Teck was led away for his lunch, and Edmund and Fran were left alone. She spoke out of a long silence.

"No wonder you wanted to keep us out," she said.

"I didn't—"

"Yes, you did. And why not? If I lived here, I'd stand at the entrance with a flaming sword, too. Do you always come by yourself?"

"Yes. What," he asked, "is the history of the twenty-seven-pound car?"

"The car? Oh, I bought it because I was crazy, I suppose. But wouldn't you have done? We were offered free passages on a tramp steamer going out to Lisbon to pick up some cargo, and I thought the thing to do was buy a car and do the trip back by land. Show Belinda and Kerry the world. So I bought a map of Spain and Portugal and we spread it out on the kitchen table and decided which route we'd take—and you saw us taking it, didn't you?"

"But twenty-seven pounds..."

"It was sitting outside a garage, marked thirty. When the man finally realised I only had twenty-seven, he let me have it, and when I told the boarders, they thought I'd gone out of my mind."

"Boarders?"

"I run a boarding house."

For some moments, he was too surprised to speak.

"You don't look like a..."

"Landlady? I do when I'm on the job. You don't look the type that knows much about boarding houses and landladies. I've got six boarders: four male, two female. Three young, one a bit older and two quite old. It was one of the young ones, male, who knew this man who knew about free passages. Of course I thought a cargo boat was one of those nice new smart ones with a few pampered passengers, but it turned out to be... well, you heard Belinda. I always thought ships were clean, but you couldn't even wash properly on this one, and you couldn't

49

wash or iron clothes. I don't say we look well-groomed as a general rule, but we don't always look the tramps we do now. No wonder we frightened you off."

"You didn't—"

"Yes, we did. What job do you do?"

He answered that question and the ones that followed it regarding his age, place of birth, address, history, tastes and prospects. Her questions were as direct, as frank and as friendly as her brother's and sister's had been.

"Where," he asked at the end, adopting her technique, "is the boarding house? And where does Teck fit in?"

"Teck," she said, "is an angel from heaven. He started out as a pantry boy when my grandparents were alive and had pantry boys. When they died, he stayed with my parents and when they died, he stayed with me. The boarding house is the house my father and my grandfather and Kerry and Belinda and I were born in. It's on Campden Heights; if you don't know it, it's a single row of big houses that used to be smart and long ago became seedy. All the others are turned into flats—all but ours. The only reason we're still in it is because Teck wouldn't let me leave it. When the shop went to pieces, he—"

"Shop?"

"My mother opened one. A hat shop. Like me, she kept having ideas, and mostly, they weren't good ones. When my father died, there wasn't much money; there was this capital which had been enough to live on—once, long ago. She thought that if she used it to open a hat shop, she'd make a fortune. She would have done, too, if she'd been able to open it in the right district—the sort of district where people would have worn the kind of hats she made. They were what's called confections, and this time, the word means what it says: you could have eaten those hats. I used to watch her creating them: lace and tulle and flowers and delicate veils. The more she worked at them, the more fragile the hats seemed to become, until at last I'd hardly dare to handle them. White, and palest, palest lavender, and sugar-pink. Campden Town admired them, but didn't buy them, and the shop went down the drain—not at once, which would have been a better way, but slowly. And then Teck couldn't bear it any longer, because he loved us all and he felt responsible for us after my father died, and as he had no money of his own to save the shop, he got desperate and tried to get some of somebody else's. He wasn't good at it, never having had any practice, and he got caught. As he's in your house, I have to tell you that he went to prison for four months—false pretenses. It's something he makes me tell the boarders before they decide to come—and after one look at him, they come anyway. He went to prison for trying to help my mother. She died while he was there, and I went to meet him when he came out. Have you ever been to meet a prisoner coming out?"

"No."

"Don't. I took Teck home and we talked over what we'd do. He offered to go away because of what he called the stigma, but I made him understand that we couldn't get on without him. It was his idea to sell the good furniture to pay off my mother's debts, and to buy cheap furniture and keep the house and take in boarders. So that's what we did and that's what we're doing. End of life history. Any questions?"

There were many, but he decided not to ask them. She was going too fast for him. He had never met anyone who leapt so lightly, so swiftly and so effortlessly over the approaches to friendship. Or who could, after an hour at a stranger's house, succeed in looking as though she had lived in it for years. She gave him the odd and not very welcome feeling that he had stepped into the wrong train and was being borne at express speed into strange and unknown country.

He had taken her for less than her age, which he now knew to be twenty-three; her casual, carefree manner must, he thought, lead many people into the same error. She was, he summed up, totally unlike any girl he had ever met.

He was brought out of his musing by a shriek he was beginning to know: Belinda was racing towards them, shouting as she came.

"Mr. Forth! Mr. Forth! *Horses!*"

She stopped beside him, breathless. In the silence could be heard the tinkle of bells.

"Can you hear?" she asked. "They're down there—ten of them. Can I ride one? Can I?"

"If you want to," he said. "Do you like riding?"

"I don't know yet. What'll I do—go down and ask the man to let me?"

"You want to ride now?"

"Yes, please—could I?"

"Does Kerry want to?"

Kerry didn't want to. Edmund gave an order, and ten minutes later a saddled mare stood outside the house, at its head the fat little Manuel. Teck and Kerry, Fran and Edmund stood waiting for Belinda to mount.

"Go on—your steed's waiting," Kerry told her. "I'm waiting, too. This I'm going to enjoy. What's the matter— lost your nerve?"

"No, I haven't," Belinda said indignantly. "It just looks" —she glanced appealingly at Edmund—"well, it sort of looks too big, in a way."

"It'll look a lot bigger when you're sitting on it," said Kerry. "Go on—what're you waiting for? A ladder?"

"What do I do?" she asked Edmund.

He went up to her.

"You mount like this—no, on this side. Turn away from the horse's head and—no, turn the stirrup—so. I'll give you a lift up—there. Now you're on. When you've gained a bit of confidence I'll take you out on a leading rein."

"C-couldn't you come now?"

"I think it would be better if you let Manuel lead you down to the soft ground."

"You'll need soft ground, and lots of it," said Fran.

"Won't you come with me, Fran? You could ride once, Fran. You said so. Come with me, Fran."

"Not me," said Fran. "I always thought it was an overrated sport. If he gets uppity, hold on to his hair."

"It's a she," Belinda pointed out.

"Then there ought to be more hair to hang on to," said Fran.

"Elbows in, back straight; grip with your knees," said Edmund.

"And with your teeth too," advised Kerry. "Shall I give him the go-ahead?"

"You keep away," shouted Belinda in panic. She swallowed hard, took the reins from Edmund and was led by Manuel down the slope. The others lined the ridge to watch her prowess.

It was not by any standards spectacular. For a time, she was content to be led round in a circle; then, moved by boredom or by over-confidence, or perhaps anxious to show the spectators what she could do, she elected to go round unescorted.

The next half-hour was full of action, but not on the part of the mare, whose sole function appeared to be waiting for its rider to be hoisted up again by Manuel. He had never known, Kerry said between shouts of laughter, that there were so many ways of falling off a horse.

But before exhaustion set in, Belinda, yelling in triumph, had managed not only to stay on, but to stay on when the mare broke into a trot. Her action was unorthodox, but she was in the saddle, and stayed in the saddle.

The next morning, there were four saddled mares waiting outside the house at what Fran called the firing-squad hour of six-thirty.

"Why before breakfast?" she had asked Edmund the evening before.

"Because it's the best time. It's cool and it's far more pleasant than later in the day. Some people get up regularly at six-thirty."

"And I'm one of the people," she told him. "But I'm on holiday."

They were walking up and down in front of the house; Belinda and Kerry had gone to bed directly after dinner, and Teck had soon followed them. In the kitchen, dark figures were silhouetted against the firelight as the servants sat round the embers eating their meal.

"Why get up so early?" Edmund asked.

"Because before a long, hard day's work, I like a nice quiet half hour to myself, having my coffee. I won't even have Teck in the kitchen. Getting up later's no good; there are all the breakfasts to be cooked, so I can't enjoy my own. Early in the morning, I go down to the kitchen and give the boiler a poke and make myself some coffee and some toast, and sit there with nobody to worry me—and then the papers come and I've just got time to look at the headlines before the rush starts."

"Do all the boarders go out to work?"

"One goes out looking for work. Two are retired; that leaves three who work."

It was an odd conversation, he thought, to be taking place between a man and a woman on a brilliant starry night, with the chirp of crickets coming from the blackness beyond the circle of light round the house.

"What's your fiancée's name?" she asked.

"Angela Wilde."

"Angela Wilde." She tried it over. "That's a good name, isn't it? I mean, it sounds nice, and it would look nice written down. It's funny, isn't it, how some names look much better than others in print? Pretty?"

She darted so swiftly from comment to question that he was left behind.

"Your fiancée," she explained. "We were talking about her."

Something in her tone gave him a disagreeable surprise; it sounded not unlike the one he used when talking to people he considered old or a little stupid. Doubtless she thought him old; he was old enough, he had to admit, to be father to her brother and sister—and to her, thirty-six was probably near enough to forty to make her bracket him with the one-foot- in-the-graves.

"I think you could say she was pretty," he said.

"How could I say so? I've never seen her. Brainy?"

"Yes."

"Job?"

"She's on the staff of a newspaper."

"Woman's page or something?"

"Editorial."

"Does she live with her mother, or with other girls?"

"She lives with her mother."

"Whereabouts?"

"In Lowndes Square."

He heard her whistle—this time, softly.

"You mean she earns enough to support her mother in Lowndes Square? Or has her mother got bags of the stuff? Don't answer that. That's a question my mother would have called inadmissable."

"Did everything go into the hat shop?" he asked.

"Yes. Bit by bit. If you ever want to know what the expression throwing good money after bad means, ask me. My father would never have let her do what she did—sell out our capital—but perhaps she'd got tired of pinching and scraping. One does. I do. I left school with the idea of getting a job and earning ten thousand a year, but the secretarial college threw me out and told me my gifts were purely domestic —which they are. Teck knew it, and that's why he knew I'd be able to run a boarding house."

There was silence for some time; he was fitting her into her background and trying to visualise her at work. He understood a little better something that had puzzled him before: the air of strength and authority beneath her light, careless manner.

"Dreaming?" she asked. "Or am I keeping you up? If I could see your face, I'd know—but it's too dark to see. You've got rather an expressive face-—did you know? It opens—and it shuts. It stays open until we do something you don't quite approve of, and then it shuts. We've made it shut several times already."

"I don't think I—"

"Oh, I'm not blaming you. Our party manners leave a lot to be desired; in fact, we haven't got any. And it must be hard for you to get the wave-length of people like us."

"To—?"

"It's hard to explain what I mean. You're what I call a *settled* person. People like you can't help getting a bit out of touch with people like us. We live in a sort of hand-to-mouth way; we balance, financially, on the very edge. For instance, when you found us stranded on the roadside, you were very kind and you fixed up the car, and then you directed us to the poo...what was that place?"

"The *pousada?*"

"Yes. Go to the *pousada,* you said, giving us what you

were sure was good advice. Well, you think the *pousada's* nice and cheap, and compared to the hotels you go to, it probably is—but for us?" She gave a gurgle of derision. "We couldn't have stayed there even for a night. Having paid the garage bill, there was nothing to do but get back to the nice free ship and get home—fast. You came to the rescue, and I'm grateful—but I'm trying to point out that people like you and people like the ones at Campden Heights don't really speak the same language."

"You're surely speaking in a purely financial sense?"

"I'm surely not. Money fixes the way we live, the way we think, the things we do, the friends we have, the places we go to, the clothes we wear—everything. People can have a certain set of values, but if they can't afford to pay for them, they have to let them go. If you look at your friends, you'll find they're people in the same income-bracket as yourself." She stretched out her arms in a yearning gesture. "Money!" she said. "Lovely, lovely money!"

"Is it so important?"

"Not to anybody who's got it. But it fills my mind all day and my dreams all night; the beat, beat, beat of the drum, drum, drum; how much is coming in, how much has to go out. One thing about having been in the red is that it leaves you with a determination never, never, never to be in the red again. When my mother died, I think she took my head with her, and left an adding machine in its place. How did I get on to adding machines?"

"You were explaining that we have nothing in common."
She spoke thoughtfully.

"Well, in a way, we haven't, have we?" she asked. "You're the kindest man I ever met—kind not because you had us here, but because you had us here when you didn't want to have us here. That's what I call kindness; the easy sort doesn't mean much. But once we leave here, can you honestly think of any reason for meeting again? I can't."

"Well, that's frank enough," he said, and to his surprise heard clearly a note of resentment in his voice.

"It's true, isn't it? Any time you want to pop in and see us, do—but you won't enjoy it much. We eat with the boarders, and there's no Zefa and Laurinda and company to help. I serve at the sideboard and Teck passes round the vegetables. Come when you like, and welcome, but I can't quite see Miss Angela Wilde taking it in her stride. She might... What did that clock strike just now?"

"Half past ten."

"And you said we had to be in or on our saddles at six-thirty?"

"Yes."

"Then goodnight."

Without ceremony, she left him. He walked slowly up and down in the darkness, thinking his thoughts. But they were confused and not very agreeable ones, and he decided to go to bed. He was annoyed to find that the thoughts went with him.

When at last he slept, it was to dream that he lived in a boarding house staffed entirely by ex-prisoners, some of whom worked adding machines while the rest made sugar-pink hats.

Chapter Four

After breakfast the next morning, Kerry and Belinda went to watch the mules being shod, while Fran announced her intention of going to see Domingo's wife's new baby. Edmund led her to the house, outside which they found Joaquina seated with the baby in her arms and two toddlers playing round her feet. Preparing to act the role of interpreter, Edmund found himself standing by, forgotten, looking on at a baby session. When it was over, he walked back to the main house with Fran. The heat was all but unbearable, but the Nash family, he had learned, didn't feel the heat; the hotter it became, the more energy they seemed to generate.

"Do you," Fran asked, "want to go inside? If so, do—but I'm staying out here."

"It's far cooler inside."

"Then go and be cool—but could you first ask somebody if I could have a long, cold drink? Lemon, with heaps of sugar."

He gave the order, but he did not go inside. Drinks were brought out to the patch of shade under the acacias; on the point of sending for chairs, he found Fran settling herself comfortably against a tree trunk. With somewhat exaggerated slowness, he lowered himself to sit beside her.

"You keep doing that," she said.

"Doing what?"

"Giving a general impression of being a hundred and forty. Why?"

"At thirty-six," he said, "one doesn't find that sitting in the heat on a dusty patch of earth on bone-hard ground is as comfortable as leaning back in a decent chair where it's cool. And in the company of you and your brother and sister, I don't really feel that thirty-six is the spring of life."

"We make you feel old?"

"Very old. I rather got the impression that you regarded me as old."

"If that 'you' is singular, you got the wrong impression. You know something? This is the first time I've ever drunk a home-grown lemon. When I get back to London, I'm going to be more productive. One day, I suppose, I'll get married and produce children, but until I do, I'm going in for vegetables. Living here, I feel ashamed of the way I've bought food without caring who grew it, or where. This is the first time I've ever thought of earth *as* earth, holding seeds and keeping them warm and giving them food until they give us food. This is the first time—Are you still with me?"

"Yes."

"Then you've got stamina. When I really get going, I find myself addressing a disappearing audience—if I've been addressing Belinda and Kerry. With the boarders, it's a case of who can get the floor and keep the floor; with one exception, they're what's called highly articulate."

"Who are the boarders?" he asked, and found her turning to look at him in surprise.

"You said that," she said, "as though you really wanted to know."

"Would I have asked if I hadn't wanted to know?"

"Being you, I suppose not. You don't go in much for merely polite enquiry. But you've given the impression, up to now, of being a bit...detached. Perhaps it's just that you're not given to asking too many questions, like us, and trying to get people's complete life history out of them in the first five minutes. It—"

"Who," he asked patiently, "are the boarders."

"Well, if you really want to know, you shall." She put down her glass. "One: Jonathon Dee, out-of-work actor. He goes out day after day, just tramping round the—"

"Two?"

"Two is Spanish. He's called Ramon, with a long string of other names after it. He came to England with a company of Spanish dancers, and when they went back, he stayed on and taught the guitar at a music school—because, as you know, there's a current craze for learning the guitar and stamping the feet and shouting Olé. He—"

"Three?"

"I do wish you'd wait for the embroidery. Three is a girl, if you call her a girl, which you probably won't, as she's about thirty-five. Her name's Leonie Rimbault. Her father owns several flourishing restaurants in the French provinces and he suddenly thought it would be a good idea to start one in London—so he sent Leonie over to open it. She started it, and that's about as far as it got. It's in Century Street. A Rimbault restaurant might mean something to a provincial Frenchman, but it doesn't mean a thing to the Londoner— yet. Leonie's father's got packets of money, but he puts it all back into the business, which is where Leonie thinks it should go, too. She works at the cash desk all through lunch and all through dinner, and sits at home the rest of the time working at her English because she thinks that if only she could speak more fluently, things would look up. Perhaps you could take your friends there and—"

"Four?"

"Four is an old man of about seventy. His name's Mr. Bisley and he used to be an artist—a good artist, he says—but he got arthritis in his hands and had to give up painting. He's got a wife who's about sixty. He's bad-tempered and she's good-tempered. They've got a separate entrance, but they've also got a door into the hall, and they come in for meals. Mrs. Bisley's taking care of the house now, or I wouldn't be at Montebarca. She—"

"Six?"

"Six is the last. It isn't much fun telling you anything. Just as I—"

"Six?"

"His name's Ivor Breck. Age twenty-five, background good, but no parents and under thumb of ancient titled grandmother who sold up all their houses when he was twelve, and now lives in a Harrogate hotel, taking the waters. She's got a secretary, a companion, a nurse and a chauffeur, and all poor Ivor's got is a measly allowance that she thinks is enough because it was enough for his grandfather to manage quite well on when the dear Queen, and you know which dear Queen I mean, was alive. Ivor wanted to be a pianist, but pianists, jazz, weren't in Granny's line, so she ordered him to study law. He's not studying law. He's got a job in a fruit and vegetable shop, but Granny doesn't know."

"How can she be unaware of the fact that her grandson has ceased to study law?"

"How can you be unaware of the fact that you roll out some pretty impressive sentences? Do you think I could do it if I tried? The reason the old lady of whom we have just been speaking is unaware of the fact that her grandson is disobeying her orders to study law is that, as you are perhaps already aware, the results of the law examinations, when published, give only the names of the successful candidates.— how am I doing?"

"Not very well. I'm still waiting for an answer to my question."

"Well, the results come out, grandson's name is not included, Granny writes him a stinker and tells him to do the exam again. Simple."

"But surely, one day, she'll—"

"—die. That's what Ivor hopes, but if she finds him out before she dies, she'll change her Will and he won't get any money, which when you come to think of it, is jolly unfair, because it's monstrous that some selfish old hag can leave all her money away from her own..." She stopped. "End of boarding house saga. Still got your eyes glued to the screen?"

"Yes. Where do Kerry and Belinda go to school?"

"To the schools my father put their names down for—boarding schools, Kerry's in Kent, Belinda's in Sussex. It was touch and go whether the schools would take them after my mother died; the hat shop shook them badly, especially when it packed up, and the boarding house almost finished them off. I had to talk fast—but as you now know, it comes naturally.— Didn't you say there was a tank somewhere here?"

"There's an irrigation tank."

"Can we swim in it?"

"If you want to. I can't take you down there until this afternoon; I've promised to take Kerry down to the pig pens before lunch."

"Pig pens, sheep, poultry and orchards and bread ovens. Is it all right if I spend a lot of time in the kitchen watching them cook?"

"They'd like to have you."

"Here's Kerry looking for you."

He got to his feet; she put out a hand and he pulled her up. She went into the kitchen, and he drove with Kerry to the pig pens, and on the way tried to disentangle his impressions. He had always prided himself on having a clear head, but it did not feel clear now. He would have liked to drive in silence— but he was with a Nash, and when the Nashes were not asking questions, they were giving out information.

"What part of Chelsea d'you live in?" Kerry asked.

"Rather near the Royal Hospital. Do you know it?"

"I've seen it. I walk about a lot, and I've been round there."

"Do you like walking?"

"Only in London. I know a lot about Old London. I've got some prints of old places—old Inns and things. Where's your office?"

"In Farringdon Street."

"That's the widest street in the City of London—did you know?"

"Well, it's certainly—"

"Do you know why? Because the Fleet River ran along there. Now it's been made into a sewer. D'you know why it's called Farringdon Street?"

"I'm afraid I don't."

"It was named after William Farringdon. He was a gold-

68

smith, and he was sheriff in 1281. I suppose you know about the old Fleet Prison?"

"Yes," said Edmund, and with thankfulness saw the pig pens coming into sight. He brought the car to a stop, and Kerry forgot Old London.

"Gosh!" he exclaimed on a long, bewildered breath. "Just look!"

They had come to a vast area of cement bordered by rows of covered pens, each with its own little latched wooden door. Kerry, following Edmund through the entrance gate, stood on the cement floor and stared about him.

In each pen was a family of tiny, pink, bald pigs, not more than a few weeks old. The man in charge of the pens opened one of the doors and lifted out two squealing, wriggling occupants and was about to give them to Kerry to hold, when the sound of snuffling coming slowly nearer, made him clap the piglets back into their pens. Edmund took Kerry's arm and drew him into shelter behind the gate—none too soon. Through it, a moment later, came an army of fat sows—and at their entrance, bedlam broke out. High-pitched squeals from hundreds of hungry throats rose from the pens and filled the air. The sows were making unhesitatingly for their own families, raising the latch of the pen with their snouts, and vanishing inside. The clamour lessened and then stilled, halving an unearthly silence—broken a moment later by angry outcries and the emergence of two sows from the wrong pens. This contretemps over, silence fell once more.

Kerry looked up at Edmund, but for once found nothing to say. The drive home was a silent one, but at lunch, his powers of speech returned and he gave a lecture on pigs to the attentive Belinda.

After lunch pigs were forgotten in the enthralling pastime of building two little cork houses; neither Kerry nor Belinda could be persuaded to leave them for a swim.

Edmund drove to the tank with Fran. He came out and dressed after a reasonable time, but she was not to be induced to leave the cool water. Floating, motionless, she gazed up at the steel-blue sky and spoke lazily.

"Is it true that the mother pigs open their own doors?"

"Quite true."

"And is it true that when grain is thrown up from the threshing floor, the wind sends a shower of gold one way and a shower of silvery-white another?"

"Quite true. Who said that?"

"Belinda Nash. And now their cork houses. Shall I go into Elvas and damage the car some more, so's we can stay here longer?" She paddled in a half-circle and eyed him thoughtfully. "I've been asking myself whether, if I owned Montebarca, I'd be able to leave it, as you do."

"What was the answer?"

"None. If you've got a business to run, you have to run it. Does this place make you a lot of money?"

"No. The cork brings in a good bit—it's cut every nine

years or so. The grapes are a loss."

"Could you afford to live here when you're married?"

"Yes. But I'm pretty sure that Angela wouldn't want to live here."

"Then when you go back, give her my love and tell her I think she's crazy. Think of one's children growing up here! Instead of a starchy English nanny, all hygiene and devotion to duty, you'd have Deolinda and Valeria and Manuela all ready to adore the babies and take care of them. I can't think of anything nicer. If I had to be a baby again, I'd be one here. And a wife, too."

"You might miss some of the things you've got used to in England."

"Such as what, for instance?"

"A telephone?"

"One of the wonderful things about this visit has been this lovely cut-off, no-beastly-phone feeling."

"Television?"

"*Television*!" A foot came out of the water and waved contemptuously in the air. "Instead of all this?"

"Well, modern plumbing, then."

"Perhaps—but with four people in charge of water, hot or cold, who'd miss taps? What else?"

"Company."

"Well, if Angela came here, she'd have you and the babies. But there's your job in London, and I suppose you'd want to go and do it. Did you always want to be an architect?"

"No."

"Did your father make you?"

"No, he didn't. But I showed promise, and it's always nice to be able to put your son into the family firm."

"If there hadn't been a family firm, what would you have done?"

"Farming. But don't run away with the idea that farming out here has any relation to farming at home. It took me years to get the hang of Montebarca."

"But you've got the hang now?"

"Just about."

"Then it's a pity to have to go back and shut yourself up in an office and tell old ladies how many bedrooms they can fit in on the site. Those that have, don't want; those that want, don't get. My mother said that the don't-gets have all the character. I must be practically all character.—What's the time?"

"Ten to four."

"Ten to four...At home, I'd be sweeping floors."

"Isn't that rather an odd time to do the sweeping?"

"It's the only time to do the sweeping. What other time is there? Eight o'clock, breakfast for the boarders. Nine, air the rooms, clear the breakfast things and leave them in the kitchen for Teck to wash; run some things through the washing machine, help Teck to make the beds, help Teck to tidy the house; go out and do the shopping, come back, do yesterday's ironing and get lunch for those who want it, clear it up and prepare the vegetables for dinner. Make scones or a cake for tea. After that there's time to get out the cleaner and go round all the rooms. Teck does the silver, the polishing, the mending—which I hate—and all the odd jobs."

"What comes after the cleaning?"

"Cooking the dinner. Dinner, the day's practically over and the next day you begin again from bar one. Do you wonder I'm enjoying myself here?"

He looked at her. Lying on the water, her hair streaming behind her, her lithe body straight, she looked very young indeed, and suddenly he thought that if he had a daughter, he would like her to look, to sound, to be just like this girl.

"Is your name Frances?" he asked her.

She spoke without moving.

"It is *not*. My name is Francesca Rosamund Annabelle, and I can't think of prettier names—and so I get called Fran."

Francesca Rosamund Annabelle. Young and vital and by any standards attractive. A thought struck him, and with uncharacteristic impulsiveness, he gave voice to it.

"With a number of young men in the house—" he began, and paused.

"Romance?" she asked lazily. "If a boarder gets romantic ideas, I throw him out. It's a big house, but it's not big enough for evasive tactics, and I've got too much to do to cope with warm blood unless mine warms up too, which it hasn't done yet. Had I got right through the day's routine?"

"You hadn't mentioned what happened after dinner."

"Letter-writing to Kerry and Belinda, if they're away. Television, depending. Music, if the musical boarders are in the mood. Do you like music?"

"Some music."

"Can you take the real moderns—in jazz or the other kind?"

"I'm not, on the whole, musical."

"That means you can't. You wouldn't like our house. Ramon with his guitar, Ivor with his jazz and Mr. Bisley with his records. Teck's a music-lover, too; he wants to start a movement to revive the old ballads. He—" She broke off and stood up in the water. "Where is he, by the way?"

"Teck? When I last saw him, just after lunch, he was walking down with Bruno to have a look at the wine lodge."

"Oh." He saw with surprise that she was looking worried. "Bruno won't ply him, will he?"

"Ply him?"

"Won't give him any wine, I mean."

"I daresay he'll ask him to sample some of—"

With one easy movement she had put her hands on the side of the tank and lifted herself out of the water. She dropped on her feet beside him, snatching a towel from the ground and beginning to dry herself vigorously.

"What's the hurry?" he asked.

"The hurry is to get to the wine lodge before Teck gets outside too many samples." She was draped in the towel, its ends held in her teeth, performing a swift, deft toilet behind its folds. She emerged to do up the zip of her dress, put on a belt and draw a comb hastily through her hair. "Let's go."

He drove her to the wine lodge. The great wooden door was closed and locked.

"Nobody," reported Edmund. "He must have gone back to the house. We'll—"

"There he is," broke in Fran, and pointed.

Ahead, proceeding slowly and not quite steadily along the scorching, dusty road, Edmund saw a broad figure.

"Come on," Fran said. "It's my fault. I should have re-membered."

Edmund started the engine, and apprehension filled his mind.

"Does he drink heavily?" he asked.

"He doesn't drink at all. He can't. He's one of those peo-ple who have to keep off it altogether. He was born without a head. Keeping away from it is no problem for him, because he doesn't like it—but sometimes, and this was one of the times, he finds that politeness demands taking a little. Slow down, will you? Stop just a bit ahead of him."

He stopped the car at the place she indicated, and switched off the engine. They got out and walked back a few paces.

Teck had lost none of his dignity. Seeing them, he came to

75

a stop and spoke in a grave, low voice.

> " *'And they would go and kiss dead Caesar's wounds*
> *And dip their napkins in his sacred blood,*
> *Yea, beg a—' "*

"That's all right, Teck," Fran said soothingly. "Come on; we'll have you in bed in no time.—Take his other arm, will you?" she asked Edmund.

" *'I saw the woman drunken with the blood of the saints','*"

whispered Teck, as Edmund helped him into the car.

"Yes, yes," Fran said gently. "In you go, Teck."

" *'Herminius smote Mamilius','*" Teck told them, standing in the car and gazing mournfully over the countryside.

> " *'Through breast-plate and through breast*
> *And fast flowed out the purple blood*
> *Over the purple vest.' "*

"Move over, Teck, and let Mr. Forth come in. That's right." She settled him beside Edmund and got into the car. "Home, please," she said.

"Does it always take him like this?" Edmund asked.

"Always. Wasn't it Oscar Wilde who said that blood and wine are red? I suppose that's the connection. But when I say always, this is the second time in three years. The last time was on my birthday, when one of the boarders thought he was just being shy, and made him join in the toast to me. It's a pity he doesn't enjoy it more, isn't it? Wine ought to go with women and song, not with all this gore and anguish."

They were at the house, and to Edmund's relief, there were no spectators.

"Shall I take him in?" he asked.

"He doesn't want taking; he just goes. He never gives any trouble; all he does is get a bit unsteady on his legs, and go on saying Blood, blood, beautiful blood."

They pushed the wooden beads aside; Teck, quietly and still with dignity, accompanied them to his room. He sat on the bed and Fran stooped and removed his shoes; then he lay back, his eyes closed, his expression peaceful.

"'It is gone,'" he murmured, "'that sensibility of principle, that chastity of honour, which felt a stain like a wound.'"

"Edmund Burke: Reflections on the Revolution in France," said Fran. "I look it all up when he's gone to sleep."

Teck was breathing deeply. Fran drew Edmund out of the room.

"Now he'll be out for an hour or two, and then he'll wake with a nice blank mind. And no hangover."

"You mean he remembers nothing of—"

"Nothing whatsoever. He thinks he was overcome by the heat, or by unusual tiredness, and I don't disabuse him. I'm sorry you got mixed up in it."

At dinner, Teck was behind Edmund's chair as usual, as grave, as quiet, as dignified as ever.

A few days later, Tia Maria-Jesus packed a picnic basket for them and they clambered on to a mule cart and went down to the vineyards to watch the picking of the grapes. In the evening they walked down to the wine lodge to watch the loaded tubs being emptied into the great stone treading tanks, and then went slowly back to the house in the dusk, Edmund and Fran behind, the children ahead.

"It'll be awful when we have to leave," Belinda said in forlorn tones. She walked backwards to question Fran. "How long more?" she asked.

"Five days," Fran said.

Both children halted in dismay.

"Five?" wailed Belinda. "Only five?"

"Seven," Kerry said. "We've only been here a week, and you said—"

"I'm allowing two days for emergencies," Fran said. "If we get to Lisbon without trouble, it means two days extra on the ship, but at least it'll mean that we don't miss it."

There was silence until they reached the house, Edmund, like the children, facing the fact of the inevitable departure. He wondered how much he would miss them. He had dreaded their coming, but their visit had brought nothing but pleasure to everybody on the estate. They had made many friends, and they had done something more: they had communicated everywhere their own enjoyment and happiness.

It had been a pleasant interlude—but like friendships

made on board a liner, he reflected, it owed most of its warmth to an enforced proximity, or propinquity, and would not long survive the end of the journey. Sensible people said goodbye —and went their way. But it had certainly been a happy time. So happy, that it was a pity it ended in disagreement.

It happened so quickly that he was at a loss, afterwards, to trace its beginning. It was after dinner on their last night. The children had had a heavy day and had gone to bed early; Teck was doing the packing; Edmund and Fran were left sitting over a map spread on a table, and he was briefing her as to the best route to take next day. The black car had been brought from Elvas and he had offered to drive part of the way with them, and Fran had given a decisive refusal.

"No," she said. "When we go, we go; we'll drive out of here and after that, we're on our own. I'll take it slowly and I'll stick to the main road, and after this, if anybody offers me a good price for the vehicle, I'll take twenty-seven pounds cash."

"You'd be wise," he said.

"I'd be lucky. And if you think we can ever thank you for the wonderful time you've given us here..."

"It was nice to have you. I only wish you'd agreed to do a bit of sight-seeing. None of you would—"

"—leave Montebarca. Well, we've got to leave it tomorrow, but we'll never forget it."

And then the telegram had been brought in and handed to

him, and she had waited while he opened and read it.

"Not bad news?" she asked.

He was frowning. He glanced at his watch; it was too late to think of answering tonight.

"No, not bad news," he said. "It's from an uncle of mine."

"Have you got to go home?"

"No. He wrote to me before I left England and I meant to send an answer from here—and forgot. It went completely out of my mind."

"Was it very important?"

"No. Well, yes, in a way. I shouldn't have forgotten it. He asked me to have two old cousins, and I meant to write and tell him I couldn't."

"You mean because you're staying here?"

"No, not exactly. It's really because they're rather a difficult pair."

"As how?"

"They were out in India for a long time—about forty-five years, I think. One of them—Louisa—went out first, and her sister Frederica followed her and they opened a school for Indian children and kept it on until it became too much for them—and then they came home."

"Louisa and Frederica... How old?"

"Well, round about the seventies, I suppose. They came home about four years ago."

"Where do they live?"

80

She had turned from the map and was sitting with her elbows on the table, her chin resting on her hands.

"That's the trouble," he said. "They don't live anywhere."

"They must have a *base* of some sort. Everybody has."

"Well, they haven't. They had a house for a time when they first came back to England—in Surrey, I think—but they had to give it up."

"Why?"

"Because they didn't understand how much things had changed while they'd been away. They bought a big, ugly place, my uncle said, that the agents were only too glad to get rid of—and then they found that it was impossible to get anybody to run it."

"And so?"

"And so they had to sell it again, but of course they couldn't get anything like the price they gave for it—and after that, they didn't have an income large enough to live on. My Uncle Robert went down to visit them and found the sale going on, and he thought the best thing to do was have them to stay for a bit, so he did. It wasn't a success. Other relations had them after that, but those visits weren't a success either. It was always understood that one day, they'd find a little cottage somewhere and settle in it, but somehow all that happened was that they began this series of visits round the family."

"For four years?"

"More or less."

"But why can't you have them?"

"For one thing, because I'm a man living alone and—"

"But didn't you say you had a married couple looking after you?"

"It isn't easy for a bachelor to take on two old ladies and—"

"But they're your cousins."

"Very distant cousins. I talked it over with my fiancée before I left, and we agreed—"

"—not to have them?"

"Yes. Once they're in, it would be pretty hard to get them out, and it would be awkward if they were still there when I was making arrangements for my wedding."

"But you said you had an empty flat downstairs—why don't you put them into that?"

He stared at her in amazement.

"Put them...you mean give them the flat?"

"Well, obviously they can't pay you much. You could charge them a sort of nominal rent, and they'd live there and look after themselves and make themselves eggs and things to eat, and they wouldn't worry you at all, and you'd be doing a lot of good."

"You make it sound very simple—but I don't think my fiancée would be quite prepared to take them on permanently."

"Why not? Because they'll get older and want looking after?"

"That's one thing. For another, they have a reputation for making trouble."

"What kind of trouble?"

"Well, they haven't shown much appreciation of all that's been done for them. Some people can pay visits without making nuisances of themselves—but that wasn't their way."

"But when you tell your uncle you won't have them, where'll he put them?"

"There are nice, comfortable homes to which old people—"

"An institution!"

"Not at all." He was getting angry. "There are perfectly comfortable houses in the country where—"

"But if you gave them the flat, how could it hurt you? You didn't want to rent the flat—you said so. You said your fiancée was going to put guests into it."

"I certainly don't see my way to installing two old women I've never seen in a flat which I've just converted at great expense."

He was growing angrier. He was aware that he was putting things in a way that represented him in a selfish light, but this girl, he thought irritably, didn't give one time to phrase anything properly; she raced on, question and answer, question and answer, until the thing had been twisted into a new and ugly shape.

"Why is this the first time your uncle has asked you to put

them up?" she was asking.

"Because up to now, I suppose, there were always people—married relations—who'd agree to have them. I can assure you we're all normally reasonable and kind people; if nobody wants them any more, it's simply because they've made themselves disliked. Now he writes to me—" He stopped. "I don't think discussing this is very profitable."

"Why not? I hate not to understand things, and I don't understand this. Look how kind you were to us. You didn't want us, but you swallowed hard, and there we were—and the reward was that it turned out well, and we'll always remember your kindness, and remember Montebarca, which is only one step from Heaven. If you can do that for us—two noisy children and an old man and me—why can't you take a chance on Louisa and Frederica? Where's the harm? If you were poor, you couldn't do it—but you're not poor. Anyway, the poor always seem to help the poor. Why do you insult your fiancée by making out that she'd rather keep that flat for guests than for two old ladies who really need it? If there'd been a phone here, you could have picked it up and got through to her and she'd have told you like a shot to have them. She—"

"I've told you that I discussed this matter with her before I left England, and her views are the same as my own."

"I don't believe it." She spoke hotly. "If those are her views, then she's a stinker and you ought to—"

"Would you most kindly oblige me by not referring to—"

"Perhaps what you *meant* to say was that your views were

84

the same as hers, by which I mean that if she didn't think you ought to have the old ladies—which I don't for one moment believe—then she talked you into not having them—and you mustn't, you mustn't, you *mustn't* let a woman talk you into anything. You *mustn't.* Don't I know what I'm talking about? Wouldn't my father, if he'd been alive now, have been able to tell you that some women can make you think anything and do anything—if you let them. What you have to do—what the man has to do because that's his job—is to listen, and only give in when it's right to give in. Look what my mother would've talked my father into, if he hadn't been calm and sensible and steady and kept his head. When he died, there wasn't any-body to stop her, and look where she landed! You're a man, and a sensible man, and you've got to go back to Angela and say: 'Look, Angela, these two poor old girls are stranded, and we've got room at the Inn'—see? And if she doesn't see it that way at first, you've got to make her, because—"

"I'd be very glad if you would kindly—"

"—-because if you *don't* do it, if you don't have the poor old things, you'll both feel terrible for the rest of your lives—and how could you bear that? Send a wire off in the morning and tell Angela you've changed your...changed her mind."

He had risen and was standing looking down at her, his expression set and angry.

"Have you finished?" he asked.

She stared up at him for some time without moving.

"You're angry!" she exclaimed in surprise, at last.

85

"I find it difficult to understand why I should listen to a—"

"If you don't listen, how can you find out about other points of view? I listened to you and I know what you think: throw the old girls to the dogs. Well, if I thought you were *like* that, I'd let the whole thing drop—but you're not like that. You're *kind;* what's more, you're kind even when what I suppose you call your better judgment tells you not to be kind. You could've asked us to come here the first time you met us—but you didn't and you were quite right: we could get along by ourselves and that let you out. The next time, you still didn't want us, and who can blame you? How were you to know what we'd all been through on that filthy ship, and what cargo decks had done to our luggage? You thought we were a bunch of ruffians, but you felt you had a sort of duty—not to us, but to yourself. So you brought us here, and as I told you before: we'll all remember it as long as we live. Now you've got the same duty—not to the old cousins, but to yourself, and if I didn't like you, I wouldn't care whether you did it or whether you didn't. But I'm in this, look; I want to go away from here tomorrow thinking of you as we all think of you now: as Edmund the Excellent. See? You've got one more chance to tell me one good reason why you can't have Louisa and Frederica.—Well?"

He made an effort and conquered his impulse to walk out of the room and leave her talking to herself.

"They are trouble-makers," he said, slowly and clearly.

"They are not, as you seem to imagine, two dear delicate old ladies in black with touches of white at the throat. They're two elderly women who for over forty years had it all their own way in India, doing, no doubt, excellent work, but doing it on their own terms; running their own affairs, getting into rather too imperious ways, and then coming back to England with the expectation of finding everybody here ready to fall in with their wishes. My family—my uncles and cousins and their children—are perfectly kind, reasonable people; almost all of them have taken the two old cousins in for a time, and without exception, every one of them has had their household disorganised, their servants antagonised and their domestic peace ruined. There was—"

"But—"

"Will you please listen to me, for a change? There was an attempt to get together and subscribe enough to buy them a little cottage. I don't say the sum raised was unduly large; one has one's commitments and putting one's hand into one's pocket for people who need never have been needy is not a thing one does with too much enthusiasm. But a sum was raised and handed over—foolishly, as we now know. My Uncle Robert should have seen to the buying of the cottage himself, but he goes abroad frequently—he's going abroad now, which is why he needs a quick answer to his question. He left the matter of buying a cottage to the two old ladies, and what did they do?"

"I'm listening."

"They decided to have a cottage built to their own design.

You can guess the rest. They by-passed architects like myself, who could have helped them and protected them; they paid over half the agreed price to a builder, and that was the last they heard of him—or the cottage. So what would you like us to do—raise another subscription? I'm sorry you don't agree with my fiancée or myself, but I assure you that I am not going to jeopardise my domestic happiness by installing two very difficult women in my flat. I shall contribute to their expenses in a high-grade and well-run home for old people—but more I will certainly not do."

He was bending over the table as he spoke, writing swiftly on the back of an envelope. He handed it to her and spoke with finality.

"When you pass through Elvas tomorrow morning," he said, "I'd be grateful if you would send that off."

She sat looking at it for some time, and then read it aloud.

" *'Regret impossible. Edmund.'* That won't cost much," she commented, and rose to her feet. "Well, all we say now is goodnight, and practically goodbye. And thank you for everything, again and again and again."

She reached up and laid her lips for a moment on his cheek—a simple and natural token of her gratitude. Then the bead curtain clattered and danced as she went out, and he was left alone.

He slept badly, and was up early, but not as early as Fran. When he came to breakfast, the suitcases were standing ready in the hall, this time held fast not by string but by their clasps, newly-mended by Teck and Rodrigo.

Breakfast was not a cheerful meal; Edmund did his best to break the silence by some remarks on the weather prospects or the probable distance they could travel in a day, but nobody sent the ball back. Kerry ate without appetite and Belinda, her eyes swollen with crying, was doing her best to keep back more tears. Fran came out of her abstraction every now and then to make enquiries about toothbrushes, slippers, or things left hanging behind doors. Nothing had been left, however; all was packed. There was nothing now but departure.

The weather had joined in the general gloom; heavy clouds hid the sun and an occasional spatter of rain dashed against the windows. Outside, in spite of this, Edmund could see figures gathering to say goodbye.

Individual farewells were clearly impossible. A way was cleared to the black car, beside which Teck was standing. Belinda looked up at Edmund and tried to speak, but tears prevented her. He took her hand and patted it awkwardly; what did one say to weeping little girls? He said nothing. Kerry was easier—a manly handshake and a brief sentence of farewell.

Fran was smiling—an unforced but rueful smile.

"The Lord giveth and the Lord taketh away," she said. "You might put an advertisement in the local paper, if there's a local paper: To Let…" She paused, her voice for a moment less than steady; then she had recovered herself. "To let, two houses of cork; fully fitted," she ended.

She was in the car. She started the engine; the faces of the two children were pressed to the windows, and then they were off, driving out of a forest of waving hands.

He turned to go into the house, and Tia Maria-Jesus hurried after him; like every other woman and some of the men present, she was wiping tears from her eyes. She handed him a crushed piece of paper which she had picked up from the ground; for a moment he thought it was the telegram he had asked Fran to despatch from Elvas.

It was not the telegram. On the paper, scrawled in Belinda's untidy, sprawling hand, was a London address: 11 Campden Heights.

She had written it down for him—but he had not asked for it. She had had it ready...

He had not asked for it.

He did not know how long he stood there, the damp, crumpled sheet of paper in his hand. He was not any longer at Montebarca; he was with a small girl who sat sobbing in a car, going back to an address for which he had not cared to ask.

Chapter Five

The next day, Montebarca returned to the serene, undeviating routine it had followed before the arrival of the Nashes. There was some heavy rain, and then the sun shone as warmly as before. Domingo came daily to the house and he and Edmund went on their rounds, talking of cork and crops. Cork buyers came and went, the lambing season began, the Moorish ploughs with their metal tips appeared behind the teams of mules. The last echoes of the visitors' voices seemed to be stilled.

But nothing, Edmund acknowledged at last, was as it had been before they came. To him, and to everybody else on the estate, their going had meant the loss of something vital.

He grew uneasy about the confusion that seemed to be closing in upon him like a fog. He had always prided himself on his orderly thinking: he liked to unroll problems on the table of his mind, study them and find exactly where the solutions lay. His difficulty now was not so much to find a solution as to decide exactly what the problem was; when he tried to think clearly, his mind went round in circles.

A longing for Angela welled up in him. He wanted to hear

her crisp, forthright, sensible sentences, he had sometimes wished her less dogmatic, more pliable, more reasonable in argument, but he had no fault to find now; he had nothing but envy for her admirable singleness of mind. She would never have allowed herself to get into the state he was in; one which he could only describe as dither, with his mind swinging helplessly between regret, relief—and remorse.

Virtue, he reflected bitterly, didn't really bring the reward claimed for it; he had picked up some people in difficulties, he had given them hospitality and a splendid holiday—and all he had got for it was an empty and dissatisfied feeling that entirely spoilt his last week at Montebarca.

Rain began to fall in earnest, pounding on the roof of the house and driving drops as big as hailstones into the thirsty soil. The baked earth in front of the houses became a sea of mud; the broad, dried-up ditches became trickles and then brooks and then rivers, and on the tracks between them, mules and oxen lurched and slithered, their hides streaming with rain.

For the first time, he left without regret. It was time to go, and he was glad to go. He wanted to get home; to get to Angela, to whom he would make a report of his adventures, and who would in three short sentences put the entire matter on a rational footing; who would take his tangled sensations and unravel them and smooth them out.

Home. Back to Mr. and Mrs. Yates and Miss Brady and Mr. Ross and Mr. Mills and old Mr. Sefton. He would return next year to Montebarca as eagerly, as swiftly as he had come three weeks before—but now that he was on his way home, he might as well acknowledge that the visit of the Nashes had in some way spoiled things this year.

He drove fast, and even if he had been in the mood to watch the scenery, he could have seen little through the ceaseless, driving rain. It came down with unrelenting force; driving his car on to the ferry that was to take him across the Tagus to Lisbon, he saw that the river, which he had last seen shimmering in sunshine, had a sulky, restless, dark-grey appearance. The hall of the lawyer's office, on his way out a refuge from the burning heat of the street, now looked dark and dank with wet, open umbrellas obstructing the entrance. The Montebarca accounts through which he had always looked with such interest now seemed to him complicated sums set in order to hold him back on his journey home.

He was up early the next morning, taking the fastest route through Spain and France and stopping only when fatigue overcame him.

London was wet—but this rain was gentle and irresolute, and he had always considered that in summer it was a tourists' city; now, in October, London had bowed farewell to her visitors and taken off her party dress and was relaxing with her own children.

He had been driving towards his own house. On an impulse, he changed his mind; he would go first to Lowndes Square. It was almost six-thirty; Angela would be home, and it was the hour with her that he most enjoyed, when they sat

93

alone in the drawing-room, their drinks on small tables by their side, and ate the olives he always brought home with him from Montebarca.

He drew up outside the house and went quickly up the steps; he was admitted, but to his surprise, he was not directed up the stairs; he was led to Lady Wilde's sitting-room on the ground floor, and asked to wait.

He glanced at his watch: almost seven. He decided that Angela had gone out, had left a message for him—and Lady Wilde would deliver it when she had finished decking herself up for whatever party she was bound for. He was tired of waiting; he would go home and change and have dinner and return.

He walked purposefully to the door—to find it opening to admit Lady Wilde.

"Oh—good evening," he said.

"Good evening." Her voice was cold, but he had never thought that she had any human warmth in her. "Please sit down."

Certainly not, he decided. He had had enough sessions with her when he had been wooing Angela; she had made him feel as if he had been bargaining for a piece of valuable property.

"I won't stay, if you don't mind," he said. "I just dropped in to see Angela."

"Really? Well, I shouldn't bother to do that any more, if I were you," she said.

He stood staring at her. She was wearing tight sage-green trousers and a wide tunic of brightly-patterned brocade. She was one of the leaders of the new vogue for casual, colourful clothes and was said to be an example to those middle-aged women who still clung to black-with-pearls, but all Edmund thought as he gazed at her was that she looked like a witch in fancy dress.

"I don't quite understand," he said at last.

"You ought to; I spoke in perfectly clear English." She walked to the sofa and sat down. "I said that you needn't bother to come round to see Angela any more. She doesn't want to see you, and asked me to tell you so."

His first astounded reaction was that she was drunk. Then he forgot her as his mind moved swiftly to another possibility: that in his absence, Angela had decided to marry somebody else. But if she had, he could see no reason why her mother should have to break the news; if there was one quality Angela possessed in abundance, it was the ability to say hard things when hard things had to be said—and even when they hadn't. She would have thought nothing of confronting him on his return and informing him, clearly and without hesitation, that she had decided not to marry him. But the idea was absurd. She was not impulsive, and if she had been considering breaking off their engagement, she would have waited until his return and given him several good reasons for her decision.

The strongest proof that nothing of the kind had occurred was his own lack of emotion; if he had really thought she had given him up, would he be standing here feeling nothing whatever but a violent dislike of her mother? It was not likely.

"Perhaps you'd better explain," he said coldly.

"Explain?" She gave the tinkling, unnatural laugh he loathed so much. "My good Edmund, the explanations, I think, will have to come from you."

"From *me?*"

She looked up at him with an angry frown.

"Look—you're not going to play the idiot boy, I hope?" she said acidly. "The whole thing fills me with disgust. I'm not going to pretend that I always see eye to eye with Angela, but this time I'm completely in agreement with her. I feel that—"

"Is Angela in?" he asked abruptly.

"She is. Don't tell me that you intend to storm your way upstairs like a wounded buffalo and break into the drawing-room. One thing at least you can do—go away quietly."

He came back from the door and made a strong effort to prevent himself from picking up her overdressed, angular figure and shaking it until the bones rattled.

"When I left England," he said as quietly as he could, "everything was all right between Angela and myself. If something's happened, I'd like to be told what it is."

She looked up at him through narrowed eyes.

"You're not drunk, are you?" she asked suspiciously.

"I may be. I probably am. I haven't had a drink today—except some wine with my lunch—but I think I must be very drunk now, because I haven't the faintest idea of what you're driving at, or even what you're talking about."

"No? Well, let me make myself quite clear. Angela wishes you to understand that she will have nothing to do with you whatsoever until you apologise fully for your behaviour—and until those women are out of the flat."

There was a long silence.

"Those women? The flat?" he asked in a dazed voice.

"Precisely." She rose abruptly. "You'll forgive me, won't you, if I don't stay here any longer looking at you putting on this rather boring performance? Anything you have to say can be written down and posted, and—"

"One moment," he said, and this time it was she who turned from the door.

"Well?"

"What women, and which flat?" he asked.

She gave a long, exasperated sigh.

"Well, have it your own way. If you really want to indulge in kindergarten antics, let me ask you some questions. Did you or did you not discuss with Angela, before leaving for Portugal, the letter your Uncle Robert had sent you regarding the disposal of your two derelict cousins?"

"I did."

"Did you, or did you not agree with Angela that you could not by any possible means accommodate the two old ladies?"

"I did."

"Did you or did you not agree to write at once to your uncle and tell him this?"

"I did. But I—"

"Please." She put up a claw festooned with heavy rings. "Just answer my questions—the last one is this: why did you then allow them, without saying one word to Angela of your change of mind, to occupy the flat which, when you left, you had given her carte blanche to furnish?"

It was some moments before he could speak. Then:

"There's some mistake," he said dazedly. "I—"

"There certainly is." She opened the door. "It's always a mistake to imagine that women like Angela—or like myself, for that matter—will put up with high-handed, not to say treacherous treatment of that kind. I've given you her message: get rid of them. Until then, I'm afraid, Angela has decided to get rid of you."

He was staring at a closed door. He shook his head in the hope of clearing it, and found the fog of bewilderment thickening. He gazed round at the chairs and tables, failed to find any answer on their expensive gold-damask surfaces, and turned and wrenched open the door.

At the foot of the stairs he hesitated, looking up. It was madness to leave without seeing her. He would go up there and—

He became aware that the front door had opened, and a maid was waiting for him to leave. She handed him a small, neatly-wrapped package, and he did not need to ask what it was.

She had sent her mother with an ultimatum—and a maid with his ring.

One had to remain calm. It didn't do to lose one's head. Having told himself this, he continued to shake with anger of a kind he had never experienced before. Hate filled him— for the green-trousered witch who had spoken so insolently, for the woman who had allowed him to be met and interviewed like a truant schoolboy.

As he drove homeward, he grew cooler. Beside him, on the leather seat, was the little package. She had given...sent it back to him—why? Because he had left his message to his Uncle Robert too late, and Uncle Robert, only too eager to seize a loophole on the eve of his departure abroad, had decided to take silence for consent. He had, no doubt, called at the Chelsea house; he had seen the flat; perhaps Yates had even shown him over it. He had succumbed to the temptation of shepherding his troublesome charges into the first place in which it would be impossible for them to annoy anybody. An empty flat; two troublesome old women...it was almost too easy.

So they were in, and perhaps Angela could not be blamed for blaming him. She had furnished—if there had been time to furnish—the flat, and all her planning and all her trouble had gone for nothing.

They were in the flat; how to get them out was something

he would have to decide later. They were in, and Fran Nash, if she had known, would have said that it served him right.

He reached the house. Through his bewilderment, anger and misery he could still look with pleasure at the neat, white building, still look forward to the quiet welcome of Mr. and Mrs. Yates, to relaxing in comfort, his needs anticipated, his habits known and respected.

He got out of the car and walked to his front steps—and then stopped to gaze down in astonishment at the entrance to the flat.

It had been a bleak area entrance, and he had used flag-stones and coloured tiles to create a picturesque little court-yard. Staring down, he saw hanging outside one of the windows a canary in a cage. A row of flowerpots stood on each window sill, with plants peeping above the soil. A kitten, coal black, was washing itself between two of the pots. There were two empty milk bottles on the doorstep, with a note beside them. There was something else, and on this his mesmerised gaze fixed itself while morbid thoughts raced in his mind: a neat little board fixed to the railing, and on the board neat hand-painted names:

Miss Louisa Forth
Miss Frederica Forth

He would have liked to move, to go indoors, to pour himself a stiff drink—or put his head under the cold tap. He was no doubt suffering from hallucinations—but even nightmares could be terrifying, and in this nightmare he was realising, with emotions that all but swamped his self-control, that all the signs—the canary, the kitten, the plants and the name-board—pointed grimly in one direction: to permanency.

They were here—to stay. If he wanted to get rid of them, it was not going to be a case of asking two old ladies to leave. It would be...it would be...he drew a deep and painful breath, and faced the worst: it would be breaking up a home.

He walked falteringly up the first step that led to his own part of the house—and was halted by a sharp command.

"Hey there!"

He turned, stepped down to the pavement and waited. The voice came from the direction he had known it would come: from below.

"I say—you there!"

He looked down. A window had been opened, and a white- haired woman with a red face, pendulous cheeks and narrowed, keen grey eyes was peering up at him.

"You won't find anybody there, you know," she said in a loud and authoritative tone. "I'm afraid Mr. Forth is away."

He found himself clinging to the railings, addressing her in a voice he scarcely recognised as his own.

"I am Mr. Forth," he said.

He had meant to sound cool. No, not cool; warm; warm with outrage. He had meant to begin as he meant to go on: by making them understand that this arrangement, made by an

101

uncle now past forgiveness, could not, would not last long.

But his words, in whatever tone they had been uttered, had caused bedlam to break out below. The head had vanished, and excited voices rose to his ears.

"Freddie! He's here! Freddie, where are you? He's *here!* No, no, not out there, Freddie—up there! I *told* you that this was the day, didn't I? Freddie, don't push ! Slowly, *slowly*; don't move that heavy thing by yourself. Now, one, two, three...Freddie, you'd better come this side; it's less awkward to hold. Now...one, two, three...heave!"

There was a crash and a cry.

"There! Look what you've done! Where shall we ever be able to get another one like that? Freddie, you are a naughty little thing. Now take this—no, no, not *that,* dear; This. Now where's the key? Hall table? Well, it isn't there now. Freddie, you really are...Oh, here it is.... That's where you're wrong, dear; it wasn't. It was *under* the hall table. Quickly, quickly, or poor Edmund will get tired of waiting out there. Come!"

The door opened. Two figures, one stout, one thin, came hastily out and hurried up the stairs.

"Dear boy!" shouted Louisa. "Oh, dear, dear boy! You're home safe at last! You're...Freddie, don't push!"

He was out of Louisa's soft, cushiony embrace and he was being pressed to Frederica's bony front. His hands were seized and he was being led down the steps and the two were pushing him before them into the little hall.

"Come in, come in, come IN!" shouted Louisa in an ecstasy of delighted welcome. "Oh, how glad we are to see you, to thank you, to bless you! Home at last, I said to Freddie, when your uncle brought us through that door. Didn't I, Freddie? I said how clever, to make a beautiful home for us out of a basement, and all so nice and light and airy! I was so frightened when Robert told us about it! I thought it was another dreadful hole, like the one the Barry Forths put us in in Cumberland, so cold, so clammy! We...Edmund, why are you standing? Sit down, sit down, sit *down,* dear boy. This is your own home, whenever you want to come into it. Sit down and tell us what you think of it. Isn't it COSY? Freddie and I had given up all hope; all. We'd said goodbye to all our dear little rugs, and our little brass-topped tables and our dear little Kashmiri cake stand, and—"

She paused. A sound had broken through her enthusiastic speech: a sound that Edmund had taken for the whirring of a cuckoo clock about to strike—but it came, he saw, from Frederica, who, plucking at her sister's sleeve, was getting ready to say something.

Louisa regarded her with kindness.

"Speak up, dear," she said encouragingly. "She's so shy," she explained in a loud aside to Edmund. "She never would push herself forward, dear little Freddie. Speak up, Freddie, what is it?"

"You haven't," piped Freddie in a high, thin voice, "told him to look at my—"

103

"Your lovely, lovely water colours! Look, Edmund; do LOOK."

He was looking, with a curious feeling of having seen them before. It did not need undue keenness of observation to see exactly where Angela's plan had given way to Louisa and Frederica's. Half the furniture was upholstered; the rest consisted of bamboo or basket work. On the walls hung Freddie's wishy-washy reproductions of a beautiful and colourful country; the *dhobi* washing clothes in a stream; a banyan tree; native craft on the Hugli. Two-tone; brown for the tree-trunk and the *dhobi*'s trunk and the boats, green for the clothes and the river and the leaves. Swati rugs covered all the floor and one of the walls, while the bookshelves housed rows of Bhuddas, ebony elephants, ivory rickshaws and a number of warnings to amateur potters.

The tenants were as strongly contrasted as the furniture. Louisa was the big one and Freddie was the little one. Louisa was...billowy was the only word that came to him. Louisa billowed and Freddie demonstrated what was once popularly supposed to happen to women who stayed too long in the East: excessive boniness, sallow, leathery skin and a parched look. Louisa had the bun and Freddie had the frizz.

They both wore black, but Louisa had the high collar while Freddie had the fichu.

"Isn't it charming?" piped Freddie. Did she pipe, or was it simply a normal voice making itself heard after Louisa's battle-cries? "I can't claim any credit; I never had Lou's genius

104

for decorating. Isn't it a good thing we were able to get rid of that girl before she put in any more heavy furniture and left us no room for our bits and pieces? We—"

"Four years!" said Louisa. "Four long years, those poor little bits and pieces, pining in store. They're as happy to be out as we are to have them out—and it's all thanks to you. Edmund dear, are you comfortable on that cane chair? You must put your feet up to get the full comfort of it—so. Then you must lie back—no, no, really back; that's right. Now isn't that better than all those old upholstered things? Isn't it the acme of comfort?"

He lay where he had been put, and listened: there was nothing else to be done.

"We're not going to attempt to thank you, Edmund," Louisa trumpeted. "It couldn't be done. You are a saint, and saints have rewards we cannot hope to give them down here. Don't think for a moment that I'm saying a word against all those kind relations who had us to stay. I'm not. But I should be telling fibs—shouldn't I, Freddie?—if I pretended that any one of them had ever really wanted us, or put themselves out to consider our comfort. There's your room, they all said, and we're so glad to see you, but you mustn't do this, and you must on no account do that, and please don't use the electric fire—why put one in a room, if it isn't to be used, I said to Freddie? - Please take breakfast in your room; it's easier for us. Please don't take breakfast in your room; the maid likes to have the dining-room cleared by half past nine. Please don't go into the kitchen; it's simpler if you don't. Please will you help in the kitchen; two people more to feed really means that I never come out of the kitchen. Please wash up. I wonder if you'd use less hot water. Can you get grease off in cold water? Can—speak up, Freddie dear."

"The worst of all," said Freddie, "was beds."

"Beds!" roared Louisa. "You call those beds? Why put us in the best spare room, I used to say, if they're going to push us into one of the servants' old rooms after a week? If it's a hint that we ought to go, why not say it outright? And where are we to go TO? Was it our fault if the price of living trebled and our income didn't? Was it our fault that a rascally builder absconded with our money, even if it really wasn't our money in a way? And then to come here and find a home! A home... but if we hadn't been firm, my dear boy, you would have had a lot of trouble with that young woman."

He sat up slowly and put his feet to the ground and wished that his head would stop whirling.

"I must say," said Louisa, "that it was very, very clever of Freddie to see what she was up to."

"Up to?" he asked.

"Freddie saw through her from the word go. Your uncle brought us here on the Thursday, and—what, dear?"

"Friday, Louisa."

"So it was. Robert brought us here on the Friday, Edmund, and by Friday evening, we had our things round us— not our bits and pieces, of course, but our suitcases unpacked and put away, and paper in all the drawers, and we'd asked your man Yates to arrange milk and bread and so on, and by Saturday afternoon, we were by way of being settled—and then this creature. Not a knock, not a ring, not a by-your- leave. The door opens, and she's in. Right in; not just in the hall, but in our drawing-room, standing there and looking as though she owned it. Freddie and I came out of the dining room—we'd just been arranging a few pieces of our Benares pottery; it looks very well, Edmund; you must look at it presently. Good afternoon, I said to her—but I wasn't cordial, I promise you. I can be as friendly as anybody else if I'm met by friendliness, but I'm not going to have any young woman less than half my age acting the Maharanee with *me*. What, I said, may I do for you? And do you know what she *said*? She said—she stood here and had the impertinence to say, right to my face: 'You can tell me what *you're* doing here.' Those very words."

"Those very words," breathed Freddie.

"When I'd got my breath back, '*doing* here?' I said—and I was very quiet, wasn't I Freddie? I said to her: '*doing* here? We are *living* here.' And what do you think she said then? She said: 'Nonsense; there's some mistake.' 'Oh?' I said—-just like that. 'Oh?' And then..."

She broke off, and an extraordinary sound, like water gurgling through pipes, filled the room; she was laughing.

"Oh dear me!" Her vast form shook. "I know I shouldn't have said it, but I really couldn't resist it."

"It was really," Freddie said, through gentle gusts of mirth, "it was really very funny. Louisa—"

"I just looked at her and said 'There isn't anything wrong with your eyesight, I hope? These are *our* things you see round you. This flat has been given to us.' She said 'Who brought you here?' And I told her that your Uncle Robert did. Then she went on to say that you had asked her to furnish the flat. 'Quite so,' I said. 'For us.' And—speak up, Freddie dear."

"And *then,*" breathed Freddie, "she...*You* tell him, Lou."

"Well, you mustn't be embarrassed, Edmund, but when she saw that this business of pretending we had no right to be here wasn't getting her anywhere, she began to bluster. She claimed—mark you, you're a very good-looking and a very eligible young man, and I daresay women have often tried it before. Who knows that when you asked her to help you with the furnishings, she didn't read more into your words than you meant to put into them? But she did take off her glove and hold out her hand with a very, very flashy ring on it, and claim to be engaged to you. 'That,' I said to her, 'my cousin will be able to confirm or deny upon his arrival, but I must tell you here and now that I cannot bring myself to believe that Edmund, who is well known in our family as a man of impeccable taste, would ask a woman to wear an engagement ring of that cheap and showy kind.'"

Six hundred and forty pounds, bought through a connection of Mr. Sefton's at a ten per cent discount...

"And she said, Edmund, that she had intended to use

this flat after her marriage to you. 'In that case,' I said to her, 'will you very kindly explain to us why Edmund instructed his uncle to offer the flat to us indefinitely, with his love?' She couldn't answer, Edmund. It was ..." She broke off abruptly and stood looking at him with a look of fear clouding her eyes. "Edmund, she...she...she isn't your fiancée, is she?"

"No," said Edmund.

"There !" Louisa's voice rang out in a paean of relief, joy and triumph. "I told you, Freddie. Have faith, I said. Believe in Edmund's generosity. You see, Freddie?"

Freddie said nothing, but her lips parted in a long, happy sigh.

"So I asked her," said Louisa, "to go away and stay away. 'If you have anything to say,' I told her, 'it can be said to my cousin when he returns from Portugal.' And then, if you please, she said that she would go on sending to the flat all the things she had ordered. 'Do,' I said to her. 'Do. I shall simply bar the door.' Which we did. Then she went upstairs, and talked to your servants. What she said to them, we don't know, but they came down here shortly afterwards—at least, the man did—and he said to me in a very rude way indeed: 'I should like to know how long you are staying.' He had to say it through the window, because Freddie and I had agreed that we were going to let nobody in until you came back. Nobody. I didn't answer at all. I just *looked* at him. And then he said, in quite a different tone: 'Madam, how long do you intend to be in residence here?' I told him that, with great kindness, you had asked us to make it our home."

"Uncle Robert asked you to make it your home?" Edmund asked.

"No, dear boy; what I meant was that you had done so. With that, he went away, and later we saw them going off in a taxi, and if only I'd realised that they'd do such a thing, I would have gone up and insisted on their leaving their trunks until you had been able to examine them. If there's anything missing, Edmund dear, I have the number of the taxi. The man said we'd given him enough trouble already—which was most unfair, Edmund, because we'd done nothing to give him the slightest trouble. Could we know by instinct where the hot water turned on? Is it too much to borrow sheets and towels until we have a chance to get our own? Is it asking too much to leave a few orders with tradesmen, or to buy one or two extra things when someone's going out in any case to do their own shopping? Can we, at our age, push heavy furniture around? Are we expected to carry down our own trunks from the pavement, where people had left them? If we run out of this or that, do you begrudge us little loans from your store cupboard? Can we help it if the postman leaves our letters there, instead of here?"

Goodbye, Mr. and Mrs. Yates. Four years of perfect service—gone.

Perhaps he was dreaming that he had been drowned and washed up on a rocky beach. The sea was surging up, receding, and then coming in again with a crash. He would wake up. It was one of those improbable incidents they kept using for plays and films: the fellow gets out of his car at his fian-cée's house and...black-out. Leads a completely different and far less pleasant life for a time, recovers his memory and there he is, still getting out of his car at his fiancée's house—but this time, everything going according to plan. Fiancée greets him warmly, hears about the family he befriended, goes out to dinner with him, finishes up at his house, and takes him into the new flat, where he congratulates her on a splendid piece of decorating. Gets back to office, begins the wedding prepa-rations, marries the girl and lives happily ever after. God save the Queen.

There were some nightmares into which you felt yourself falling...falling.... Down a pit, off a pavement; it didn't mat-ter. The thing was that you had the terrible feeling that unless you made a strenuous effort and pulled yourself out of sleep—you'd fall...and fall, and that would perhaps be death. It was difficult to do; you had to fight.

He'd caught it. It was a disease, and he'd caught it. If he didn't rouse himself....

He rose slowly to his feet and looked at the two faces turned to his. Louisa took one of his hands and spoke warmly.

"Until you get somebody else, Edmund, you must come and eat with us. Freddie makes the best curry you ever tasted, and we make our own poppadums, and our own chutney, of course—not mangoes, alas!—but tomato. I myself turn out an excellent fish kedgeree, and Freddie makes the most wonder-ful ginger wine."

111

"You said just now that I had asked you to make this your home," Edmund said slowly. "What I was wondering was...I mean, did Uncle Robert explain..."

"Explain? My dearest boy, what was there to explain? He came to us and just put it into our hands, and stood there until we'd read it, saying nothing—and we could say nothing, either. Edmund, let me be quite frank: we wept. I'm not ashamed to say so. I tried to hide it, but I knew that tears were pouring down my face, and when I looked at Freddie, there she was, howling. In heaven, my dear boy, you will get your reward for those beautiful, beautiful words."

"Thank you. I can't," said Edmund, "entirely remember the words."

"We kept them. It's here in my breast pocket and always will be," said Louisa. "It's said that telegrams bring bad news, but did ever better news come in one?"

She put the telegram into his hand, and he read it, standing on the Swati rugs. It had been sent from Elvas. It must, he thought dully, have cost her a great many escudos. It read:

Robert Forth. SEXTALEVER. London.

Regret not answered earlier please offer garden flat of my house indefinitely to Louisa and Frederica with my love.

Edmund.

Chapter Six

He would, he resolved during the next few days and long, wakeful nights, leave it at that. He would not—as had been his first violent intention—drive furiously to Campden Heights and vent his fury on her.

He would leave things as they were, and so get some measure of revenge—for, being a woman, she would want to know the sequel. So much, at least, he could deny her. She could, if she wished, come to Chelsea and look down and ascertain from the canary and the cat and the painted pots that her billeting scheme had succeeded; what she would not know, now or ever, was how he had reacted.

Office, for the first few days after his return, was a place of refuge. There he could forget himself, forget his two unwelcome guests, forget that he had taken in a stranded girl and been rewarded by treachery. In his office there was nobody who could remind him in any way of his brief acquaintance with the Nashes, or who would refer to Angela. Except, he found, Mr. Sefton.

He lived in Kensington. Edmund seldom visited him, for though Mr. Sefton, besides being his godfather, had been his father's closest friend, the association had been mainly what Edmund termed a Club one: the two men had met frequently outside the office, but seldom in one another's homes. Since his father's death, Edmund's connection with his godfather had been almost entirely in the office; he liked him, but he had never been able to decide what lay behind the mild blue eyes and the bland expression, and could never cope with the older man's sardonic utterances.

Four days after his return, Mr. Sefton had more to talk of than business matters.

"Oh, funny thing," he said casually. "I met somebody who knew your name. Ex-butler of sorts; old fellow called Teck."

Edmund looked across his desk at the stooping form and the thin, clever face, and waited. One should have known that old Sefton wouldn't be long before smelling something out, he reflected dispassionately. No wife, no children, a three-roomed furnished flat by way of home; no ties, no responsibilities outside the office, nothing much to do but wander round the locals drinking beer and picking up acquaintances—and gossip. An able fellow—professionally, a brilliant fellow—but without ambition of any kind; with a spectator's attitude to life and a genius for picking up snippets of information about people and places. Edmund had never been able to account for his father's high opinion of him.

"I put him up—and the family he was with—for a week out in Portugal," he said. "Their car broke down. Would you ask Miss Brady—"

"I know the fellow who sold them that car. He lives round my way; I was talking to him last night at a bus stop when this old fellow came up and joined us—and of course the fellow wanted to know how the car had gone, and the answer was that it hadn't, and that they'd been rescued and housed and royally entertained for a week by—guess who?"

"Myself."

"Small world. Apparently this girl who bought the car runs a kind of boarding house up at the top of Campden Heights. Nice part, that used to be; healthy, but it's gone a bit seedy. She paid twenty-seven pounds for the car: you can't wonder at its folding up. What gave way, exactly?"

"Almost everything," said Edmund.

He did not sound amused, and Mr. Sefton looked at him more closely.

"I suppose it wasn't much fun having an entire family dumped on you."

"There was room for them all."

"Well, you don't look as though you'd enjoyed it. They came home on a cargo boat of sorts. Dillon Line. I know one of their chaps, but I didn't know they had any boats you'd put human cargo into. Seen any of them since you got back?"

"No."

"Pity; they sound an enterprising lot—at least, the girl does. Name of Frances."

"Francesca Rosamund Annabelle," said Edmund, before

he could stop himself.

"Eh?"

"I just told you her names. She isn't called Frances."

Mr. Sefton took time to ponder.

"There's a bit of trouble, isn't there, between you and Angela Wilde?"

"At the moment—yes."

"Nothing to do with this Francesca Rosamund What's-her-name?"

"Nothing whatsoever."

"Oh. I just wondered. For one moment," Mr. Sefton said, "I had a hope that you'd run into something, run up against something."

"As my godfather, I can't see why that should give you any pleasure."

"As your godfather, I'm interested in your development. You're not given to confidences, so I have to fall back on my own observation, and I observed on my last visit to Lord Wilversham, who's just moved into your street, that you've got those two old cousins housed down in the new flat. I'm glad you put them there—which I didn't think you would have done on the eve of wedding Miss Wilde; I would have said her tastes didn't run to housing old ladies. Perhaps your Uncle Robert pushed you into it. If he did, you'll have difficulty in persuading him to get them out again—if you want them out again. He's been trying to slip out of that noose for years—and in the meantime he's got himself quite a useful reputation as a kindly fellow, which he isn't. He's your father's only brother, but thank God there was never any resemblance between the two of them, inside or out. I'm surprised you've always been able to stomach Robert; personally, I can't. Well, it's almost time to be off; I'm keeping you from going home."

He went out, and Edmund was left to the realisation that he didn't in the least want to go home. There was no longer an efficient Yates on the watch to have the front door open before he'd had time to put the car in the garage. The house wouldn't be warm and his clothes wouldn't be laid out and his bath wouldn't be ready. There wouldn't be drinks in the drawing-room and Angela wouldn't be looking in—or, if she didn't, he wouldn't be able to have a long telephone conversation with her with the receiver in one hand and a drink in the other.

Gone—comfort, service, gracious living. And his fiancée. She had stated her terms and she would keep to them, because that was the kind of woman she was. He had always admired the way in which she could make up her mind and stick to it. He had admired her decisiveness, her refusal to argue once her mind was made up. It seemed, at this moment, a less desirable trait than he had once thought it.

He drove home and put the car away as quietly as possible, and even more cautiously closed the garage door and walked towards his front door. One...two...three; he had never yet been able to get beyond four.

Four—and there it came.

"Edmund! Freddie dear, it's Edmund! He's home!"

He leaned over the railings.

"No thank you, Cousin Louisa. I shan't want any curry this evening. I've decided to dine out."

"Oh!" She was leaning out of the window and gazing up at him, and her voice held bitter disappointment. *"Chingree* curry, Edmund—we went out and got the most delicious prawns and—speak up, Freddie dear. Oh! I am a silly-billy, Edmund! Here I am talking about curry when that poor girl is waiting for you. Charming," she roared. "I heard someone going up to your door, and of course you know we're always on the look-out for visitors for you, ever since those wretched people deserted. I asked her to come in and wait for you here, but she wouldn't, so I took her up to your drawing-room. She came at about twenty to six, and I told her you wouldn't be long. Go in, dear boy, go in ; you should never keep a pretty girl waiting."

But he had gone up the steps and put his key in the door. She was standing at the drawing-room window, and she turned as he came in. He closed the door carefully behind him and stood waiting for her to speak.

She looked, he thought, different. No tan, perhaps. Woollens instead of cottons. Stockings instead of bare legs and shoes instead of sandals.

She was frowning, and she seemed to be staring at him

expectantly.

"Well," she said at last, and there was impatience—and more, exasperation—in her tone. "Go on—say it!"

"I've nothing to say."

He saw the colour leave her face.

"All right," she said. "I shouldn't have done it. All the way to Elvas, I thought and thought and *thought.* I know I shouldn't have done it. But... but it was *right,* don't you see? Don't you?"

"That wasn't for you to decide."

"But it was! If you'd sent that telegram yourself—and in a way I wish you had—it would have been between you—and them. But it was in *my* hand. *I* was the one who had to write the message down and send two old people into an institution. Not you—*me.* To the end of my life, I would have thought about them—and about you, because it was a sort of crisis for you, and you weren't solving it the right way."

"Have you solved it the right way? They're in residence—as you saw. And I told you that they weren't as you'd pictured them—two dear old fuddy-duddies crushed and broken by misfortune. They're worse, much worse, than my relations painted them. Nobody liked to draw too accurate a picture—after all, wasn't everyone hoping to pass them on to someone else? They hadn't been here long before they'd succeeded in driving away the best pair of servants I ever had or am ever likely to have. I engaged another couple, and after one session with Louisa and Frederica, they melted away. You could have put any other people down in that flat and perhaps they would have understood that they were to stay in it, except for occasional or emergency visits upstairs. Those two? No. They've got a key—as you saw. They use it. They tidy my rooms—rearranging them in the way they prefer. They cook curries for me. If I don't go down there and eat them, they bring them up here in something they call a tiffin carrier which they leave in the dining-room to be heated up when I come home. They keep a look-out when I'm at office and come up to see who's at my door. They—"

"They *love* you!" she broke in. "They *love* you!"

He was so astounded that for some moments he could only stare at her.

"And you...you seriously imagine," he said at last, "that their gratitude or affection makes up to me for the loss of my privacy, my comfort, my well-being, my...*my fiancée*" There was another silence, and out of it she spoke breathlessly.

"You don't mean she...she didn't... she didn't..."

"She will see me again, and accept my ring again, the moment I've got rid of the two old ladies to whom you so kindly offered my home."

"But you could have told her it wasn't your fault!"

"I couldn't have told her, unless I'd used a megaphone and shouted it to her up the stairs, which I didn't care to do."

"But *I* can tell her! If you'll only tell me where she lives and—"

She was already snatching up her mackintosh.

"That at least," he said, "you can spare me."

There was a note in his voice that halted her and made her cheeks, if possible, whiter than they were already. The echo hung in the quiet room, its weariness, its bitterness, its boredom only too clear. He went on speaking in the same tone.

"You're very young," he said, "and you're very naive. You have warm feelings which do you credit, and which no doubt make your family and your...your boarders happy. But you have not yet learnt that you're not really hand-picked by Providence to set right any matter that appears to you to be maladjusted. You should have gone on wielding your toy sword within your own circle. You should have refrained from interfering in a matter of which you knew nothing whatsoever beyond a few surface facts. In return for any small kindness I may have been able to do for you and your family, you have wrecked, temporarily at any rate, my life. What you've done can't be undone—yet. But the one thing I cannot and will not have is any further interference in my affairs. My fiancée thinks that I acted without consulting her, and she is naturally angry. Anger I am prepared to accept; ridicule I am not. I am in a difficult position, but it would be far more than difficult; it would be impossible and unbearable if it were to become known that I had been put into this position by a girl I scarcely know, who lost her head and made a fool of me."

He stopped. She was standing staring at him, and tears were pouring down her face, but she ignored them. Something

121

in him moved in protest. She looked as Belinda had looked on the morning she said goodbye to him at Montebarca, an unwanted address clutched in her hand. But there were things he had to say, and he was going to say them.

"I am not a young man," he said. "I am nearly thirty-seven. I know that you found me rather too formal; rather too stiff. I *am* rather too formal, rather too stiff; one of the things that matters rather a lot to me is my self-respect—my dignity. You have managed to make me lose a good many things. I hope you will at least leave me those."

She said nothing. Still ignoring the tears, she folded her mackintosh neatly over her arm and walked towards the door. He opened it for her in silence and accompanied her into the hall and towards the front door. He had spoken of dignity, and she had it at this moment. He felt, suddenly, helpless and frustrated. He had said what he had resolved to say—and what had been the use? It hadn't made him feel any better; he was feeling a good deal worse. He would have done better to say nothing; he could merely have asked her to leave. He talked one language and she talked another. She spoke a language that—

The language of the heart?

The phrase, leaping into his mind, stayed there and refused to be dislodged. He told himself that the words were meaningless, but he found himself wondering whether he had once understood, once spoken the language—and had forgotten it. Had he spoken it, only to find that Angela and her friends did not understand it?

There were answers to all these questions, and perhaps he would find them when she had gone....

He put out a hand to open the door—to find that she wasn't, after all, going. Not just yet. She had swung round with startling suddenness and was facing him. The tears were still falling, but her eyes were blazing with anger.

"There is nothing," she said, the words coming out with difficulty, "there is nothing in the least naive about me. And I have never once thought that I'd been hand-picked by anybody to interfere in anybody's affairs. I've run my own affairs for years—mine and my brother's and sister's and, when she was alive and after she was dead, my mother's. What do *you* know about running anything except your business, which is run for you? All you've ever had to do is reach out and help yourself to something off a plate. I listened to you out there at Monte-barca and I thought: he's never had to fight. And you haven't. You've had it all your own way and because there was something decent about you it didn't spoil you—much. All it did was give you the feeling that a lot of people like you have: that people are only poor or out-of-work or unlucky through their own fault. They didn't manage things properly, or they were extravagant—or just plain stupid. You never had to fight. You never had to make a move to get anything, and that's what's made you stiff—stiff in every joint; not outside, but inside. You're caught in your own narrow little world, and you don't know and don't care what goes on outside it. Naive? You're the one who ought to grow up. You're the—will you kindly take your hand off that door? I haven't *begun* yet. What do you know about people like those two old cousins of yours downstairs when they realise that the next stop's a room in some institution you pay the rent for? You don't know—but *I* know, because I've seen impoverished old ladies before and because, unlike you, I've done what I could to help them. Now you're shouting for help just because you've been saved from tying yourself up to a woman who sounds to me halfway between a harridan and a hell-cat. Give you a hearing? No, not she! Defer to your better judgment, if you've got better judgment? Not her! Which matters to her more? Those two downstairs, or her own... Ha! *Dignity!* She told you to do something, and what did you do? You didn't do it! Imagine! You actually did something without telling her— something kind, something decent, something fine. *That,* all that sort of stuff, doesn't interest her. All that interests her is make-him-come-to-heel-or-he'll-never-come-to-heel- again. *That,* I've saved you from—but don't take your chance while you've got it! Don't fall down on your knees and thank God I waved my little toy sword just in time; just crawl back. Don't try to see those two old women down there as human beings instead of circus exhibits. Don't, above all, don't get yourself mixed up with some crummy bunch of people who keep a boarding house somewhere in the purlieus, even though the two young ones are praying that you'll come back into their lives. Just go on the way you're going— round and round and round into your winding sheet—back into your sar-cough-agus. And now you can open the door and let me out, and don't bother to slam it behind me, because I'll do that myself."

He put out a nerveless hand towards the door, but she had swung it open and was standing outside. He flinched in anticipation, but she had something more to say.

"You needn't tell me!" she shouted. "I *know! Sarcophagus!*"

The crash shook the house. He was alone.

Chapter Seven

Edmund had not hitherto thought of a month as an unduly long period. Hamlet, he remembered, had called it a little month, proving that he too considered it not too long a stretch. But a month, he reflected, had sufficed to wreck his home and his projected marriage. Not much more than a month ago he had sat in this office chair, in which he now did so much brooding, and had watched Miss Brady tidying up— and it had occurred to him then that she seemed to be clearing up the effects of someone who had died. He was alive—but his old way of life was dead.

On balance, he thought, he oughtn't to be grumbling; he'd had perfection of a kind, and perhaps it had been too much to expect that it would continue indefinitely. Turning his chair round, he stared out at the gathering fog and wondered who was going home this evening, as once he had gone home, to a blazing fire, a well-cooked and well-served dinner and sandwiches and a decanter left in the drawing-room in case he should stay up late.

So much for home life. His love life had not so much shattered as dissolved. He had written twice to Angela; while she had not done anything so childish as returning his letters, she had given no sign of having received them.

The office was no longer a place of refuge. Mr. Sefton, perhaps sensing that there was more to be learned at Campden Heights than his godson was willing to tell him, had found his way there by way of the man who had sold the car to Fran Nash. Apart from telling Edmund of this visit, and of subsequent ones, he gave no details, and Edmund was left to fill in as he might. Of one thing he was certain: that neither Mr. Sefton nor Angela would ever learn the humiliating truth about the despatch of the telegram. Fran Nash had many qualities he considered undesirable: she was undisciplined, over-impulsive, muddle-headed and interfering beyond forgiveness—but something told him that sending the fatal telegram was a fact she would impart to nobody.

Home life, love life, office life—all changed in Hamlet's little month.

Miss Brady put a call through and he picked up the receiver and heard his Uncle Robert's voice.

"Wouldn't care to meet me at my Club for lunch today, would you, Edmund?" he asked. "Are you free?"

"Yes." There had been only the briefest hesitation. "Thanks. What time?"

He disliked his uncle's Club. Not long after entering it at lunch time, he found to his surprise that he also disliked his Uncle Robert.

His nerves, he decided, were wearing thin. He had seen the stout, well-groomed figure, the strong, clean-shaven face and rather prominent brown eyes all his life, and had found nothing in them to arouse this feeling of aversion. Perhaps it was something new in his uncle's manner. Perhaps it was only the fact that he had been chosen for this errand.

There was nothing, at first, but the usual preliminary exchanges. They were both well, thank you; yes, Uncle Robert had had a very good trip round the Chateaux country, and his wife, Aunt Olga, had enjoyed it—but they'd decided, on the whole, that October was a bit too late in the season. No tourists, which was pleasant, but a nip in the air that had tickled up your poor old aunt's sciatica; weren't getting any younger, any of us, ha ha. It was clear that Uncle Robert was feeling younger than ever, and finding it difficult to put up with poor old Olga's rapid decline.

He came to the point over the fish.

"Tell you why I rang you up. It was really because Angela's been in touch with me. She—can't think why they don't fillet this damn fish better." He made a furtive exploration of his mouth with a forefinger and removed a bone, placing it on the side of his plate and regarding it malevolently. "Looks nothing at all, but you swallow it and you'll soon find it's as sharp as a drawing pin. Damned dangerous. I'll send in a complaint—it isn't the first time."

"You were saying?"

"Oh, about Angela. She got in touch with me."

"She wrote?"

"No, she telephoned the day I came back." He finished his fish, pushing his plate away, and sat looking at his nephew with a puzzled frown. "I must say you've given her plenty of cause for complaint. After talking it over with her before you left for Portugal and deciding... Mark you, I'm not going to pretend that your telegram wasn't a godsend. Nothing more or less than a godsend. I wouldn't believe it until I'd had the thing confirmed; I thought there might be a mutilation of sorts—does happen, you know—and I couldn't have acted unless I was sure. I thought, I don't mind telling you, that you'd got a touch of the sun out there at—what's the name of the place again?"

"Montebarca."

"That's it. Well, I thought it was either sunstroke or the wine. Your poor old aunt thought I ought to wait until you came home, but I said No fear. Nothing doing; I'd had them round my neck for long enough, and it was time somebody else had a go."

"You had been very kind to them. You—"

"Kind? I should say so! If I'd known what I was letting myself in for, d'you think I'd have taken them on? No. I'd have formed a family committee right from the start, and I'd have put it to them straight: look here, I'd have said, you'll have to house these two, or as likely as not you'll have them picked up for vagrancy or getting their name—our name— into the papers for some financial straits or other. But like a fool, I didn't

129

do that; I passed 'em round in the hope of finding a permanent billet with one or other of the family. I'd had them myself for a couple of weeks, and I might have guessed from that experience that nobody'd be able to stick 'em for long. No, no." He gave a brief guffaw. "You bought it, old chap, and don't think we're not grateful. But you've got to keep the thing in proportion; I've had my turn, now it's yours. You got me out of a mess; if I hadn't had that telegram, I couldn't have gone off with poor old Olga. As I said, she thought we ought to wait until you got back, but I told her that if a fellow of thirty-six or seven shot off a clearly-worded and unambiguous telegram without giving the matter due thought first, it was time he learned. So I got straight into the car and drove off down to Sussex and picked up the two old girls and brought 'em up to London and installed 'em. Mark you, any of us would have done the same if we'd had the facilities—put 'em up permanently, I mean. But you must remember that we've all been selling off our big places and getting into these chicken coops everybody lives in nowadays. Poor relations were no problem when you could park 'em in a couple of rooms where they wouldn't get in anybody's way—but today? You can see, can't you?"

"Yes, I can see," said Edmund.

"Well, when I found you'd actually gone as far as to furnish the place, I knew you must've had the old girls in mind all the time—so you can imagine that it was a bit of a knockout to listen to Angela telling me that you'd discussed it with her before you went out to Monte...to that place, and that the two of you had definitely decided to write and advise me to find one of those last-harbour places and fix the old girls up. What made you go over Angela's head like that? You must have known she was a woman you couldn't—"

"We didn't really discuss it. I'd had your letter, and when I told Angela what you wanted, she said you couldn't have it —and at that time, I agreed with her."

"And you had a change of mind, or should I say heart? And it's lucky for me that you did—but that's not the point Angela wants me to make now. The little grievance she's nursing, and I don't blame her, is the way you rode roughshod, so to speak. Why not a telegram to her to tell her your change of plan and ask her to let me know?"

"If I'd done that, do you think she would have accepted it?"

There was a long silence. Edmund had no idea what his uncle was thinking, but his own thoughts were surprising him. The question he had just put to his uncle was one to which there could be only one answer: if he had sent a telegram announcing his change of mind to Angela, he knew with certainty that she would have thought it over coldly and calmly, decided that she had not made her own point clear enough— and she would have told his uncle that he would not accept the responsibility of the two old cousins.

Did all women interfere, each in her own way? Was the sending of the telegram from Elvas very different from the other kind of interference? One was head and one was heart, but the result was the same in both cases: a man might just as well talk to himself.

He realised with a start that his uncle must have been talking to himself for some time.

"... and of course I see your point, but you can't leave matters as they are, you know."

"You mean you're prepared to take Louisa and Frederica on again?"

"My God, no!" There was no mistaking the tone. Uncle Robert was out of this difficulty—for good. "No, I think you've done a fine thing and it's a solution that couldn't have been bettered. It was Angela I was talking about. You've hurt her and—"

"I've made her angry."

"All right; you've made her angry, and it's up to you to make things right again."

"How? She won't see me until Louisa and Frederica are out of my flat. Is she a woman who says things without meaning them?"

"No, she's not. She's an opiniated b .. . I mean," said Uncle Robert in panic, "she's got a damn fine brain and—"

"Are you on her side, or my side?"

"I'm trying to make you see that you can't throw away the chance of marriage with a girl like that —"

"But you don't like her."

132

"Have I ever said such a thing?"

"No, you haven't. It wasn't so much what you said; it was a feeling I had that—"

"Well, I might once have thought that she was a bit too high-and-mighty," his uncle acknowledged. "But that was before I realised that she had something to be high-and- mighty about; she does, after all, know every person of influence in London, and she's coming into all the Wilde money. It's... well, let's face it, shall we?" The avuncular tone had gone; this was man to man. "Let's look at it straight. You can't tell me that you didn't take it all into consideration before asking her to marry you. Oh—beauty— yes! That figure—yes, yes, yes! I'll give you all that. But you're not a boy, and if you ask me, you never were. You've always had a lot more of your father than your mother in you, and your father never missed a good chance in his life. No Forth ever does. You can't sit there and tell me that at thirty-six or seven, you didn't let your right hand know that the left hand was getting itself round one or two things like blue blood and kindred benefits. There's nothing the matter with Forth blood, but we've been in a bit of a rut for the past hundred years, and we can do with an Angela or two. Oh, I know what you're going to say! You've got all the money you both need, without having to touch hers; that's quite right. And I'm not forgetting that you're one of the most eligible and, when you get out from behind those glasses of yours, one of the best-looking men in London. But you can have Heaven, too—and married to Angela, where couldn't you

133

end up ? Nothing would stop you but the ceiling. And that's why I'm here—to patch up this silly quarrel and get the two of you together again, and no face lost."

This was really happening, Edmund thought. He was really sitting here, listening to this. And when the engagement had been announced, he'd taken Angela on a round of relations, and Uncle Robert had given them a beaming blessing and had patted Angela's hand and prophesied that they would have good-looking children....

From that—to this. Francesca Rosamund Annabelle Nash had indeed set something rolling...downhill.

"If Angela cares to put up any other proposition," he heard himself saying in a quiet voice, "I'm willing to consider it. But I can't turn Louisa and Frederica out of the flat, and I'd be glad if you'd tell her so."

He saw his uncle glaring across the table at him.

"D'you think I'm going to carry a message of that kind?" he demanded.

"Look." Edmund endeavoured to speak reasonably. "The telegram might have been a mistake. For that, I'm prepared to make an apology. But Angela knew, when she issued her ultimatum, that Louisa and Frederica were settled in my flat. Whether she liked the idea, or didn't, the fact remained: there they were. What I'd like to know is what she expects me to do—throw them out again?"

"Not at once, no. So far, I'm with you. You offered them

a home, and that's what they made it. I was down there this morning, and I could—"

"You went to the flat?"

He heard the loud guffaw which he had always thought so jovial and which now sounded like the snort of a large animal.

"Went to the flat? Not likely, my dear fellow. I've just told you—you bought it; it's yours. No, I didn't go to the flat; I'd dropped in to see Wilversham—I suppose you know Lord Wilversham's moved to the house next door to yours?"

"Mr. Sefton told me."

"Well, you ought to get in touch with him. He's likely to want quite a lot done to the house, and you ought to go and look him up and tell him you're my nephew. Don't know him well myself, but he's going to be useful when my name goes up for...did I tell you I was going into politics?"

"No."

"Well, I am. And people like Wilversham and the Wildes are going to be pretty useful, I can tell you. But on my way back this morning I passed the flat and I stopped and looked at it—cautiously, you understand? I didn't want to be caught. I saw enough to know that they've really spread themselves out. For good. And in their place, wouldn't you have done the same ? Wasn't it necessary for them to present you, on your return from Portugal, with a touching picture of the little nest they'd made there, so cosy, so neat, so sweet— and so obviously permanent? How, they'd argue, could you have the heart to turn

135

them out after seeing that—and after hearing their hymns of praise? You've got to discount all that. The advice I've got to offer you is this: take Angela to see the old girls, and in her presence, tell them that they can be there for a definite time: two months, three months, after which you're going to be married and will need the whole of your house. What's more reasonable than that?"

"Angela and I don't need the whole of the house. I never liked her idea of putting guests down there."

"Then why the hell did you go to the trouble and the expense of converting the place?"

"Because I'm an architect and it wasn't an easy conversion and I gave my mind to it in a purely professional way and as a purely professional exercise. Once it was done, of course, I realised for the first time that something or someone would have to be housed in it. And I'm grateful to you for your suggestion, but in my view, it's a perfect place for the two old cousins and I'm ashamed to think it didn't occur to me. Occur to me earlier, that is."

He saw the brown eyes staring at him, and it struck him that there was something fish-like about them.

"When I got that telegram," said Uncle Robert slowly, "I told you what I thought: sunstroke. This confirms it. What I said about being like your father: forget it. That was your mother talking, and her middle name was sentiment." He signalled to a waiter and ordered coffee. "Well, here's another proposition: why don't you ship the old girls out to that place of yours in Portugal? You'd be able to keep up this kind-to-the-poor attitude you've struck, and they'd be out of Angela's hair. When you come to think of it, that's the best solution of all. Will you agree to that?"

"No."

There was nothing fish-like about the eyes now. They were hot with fury.

"All right." Uncle Robert spoke with difficulty. "I've said my piece; now you say yours and let's get back to sanity. Come on; come on; what's the message to Angela?"

"You can give her my love and tell her that in future, I won't send telegrams without consulting her. You can also tell her that it is quite impossible for me, even if I wanted to, which I don't, to evict my cousins. You can remind her that they're no kin to her, but if she marries me, they will be. You can also tell her that now, as in the future, I can't fall in with her wishes until I've had more time than we had before I left for Portugal to put my own views before her and find out what she thinks of them. You can tell her that I have a great respect for her intelligence, but that in this instance it seems to have deserted her. You can tell her that I have never met a woman I admire and look up to more, but even from her I am not prepared to accept ultimatums, especially when they are issued through her mother. I have her ring and I shall be happy to put it on her finger again, even though she sent it back to me by a servant. Tell her, finally, that I will in all cases and at all times be interested in her views, but I do not bind myself to agree with them."

And that, he saw, was that. His uncle was purple, but this was not the place for an outburst; he would have to control himself until he could let off steam at poor old Olga.

Nothing more was said. It was evident that Uncle Robert, like Lady Catherine de Bourgh, would say no farewells and make no compliments.

They walked through the crowded dining-room and out of the Club. Only on the pavement did Uncle Robert, perhaps revived by the cold air, make his pronouncement.

"I shall simply tell her," he said savagely, "that you've gone stark, staring mad."

Chapter Eight

For the next few weeks, Edmund, who was experiencing unfamiliar sensations of loneliness, set himself to find out what had become of all his old friends. He discovered that they fell into three groups: those who had gone abroad and with whom he had lost touch; those who had married and had been gradually absorbed into family life—and those who, since his meeting with Angela, had been allowed to drift away.

His efforts to re-establish contact were not markedly successful. He paid several week-end visits to the country, played with his godchildren, built brick houses by nursery fires, and held babies while they drank their milk, but always, on his way back to town, came to the conclusion that between bachelors and family men there was a wide and unbridgeable gulf.

His attempts to round up his few bachelor friends in or around London met with an equal lack of success; they had not liked Angela and Angela had not liked them and had made it clear that when she married him she was not going to burden herself with her husband's boyhood chums.

His Club held no attractions. It was not golfing weather. All that was left was his home, and to it there came one day a very fat, very black, very cheerful couple who introduced themselves as Mr. Welty and Mrs. Euphonia Grand and explained that they had been sent by Miss Nash to work for him, if suitable. Edmund interviewed them, engaged them and found his domestic trials at an end. They sang calypsos as they cooked, but both the singing and the cooking were of a high standard. They owned a small dog called Cha-Cha, but it was well-behaved and had the endearing habit of joining Edmund by the fire of an evening and falling asleep with its paws clasped affectionately round his ankle.

"If *only*," Louisa said, when she and Frederica had come up to find out how the new couple were progressing, "if *only* we'd thought of that solution, Edmund dear. There's nothing like natives for working willingly and well. In all those years away from England, Freddie and I had no trouble at all. You must go at once and thank Miss Nash for sending them, Edmund dear. Such a *nice* girl. She—speak up, Freddie dear. Yes, I'm just going to tell him. Mr. Sefton knows her, Edmund. Did you know that he had come in to see us?"

"Yes; he told me in the office that he'd called on you. I'm sorry I didn't bring him before."

"Your godfather, *and* your father's greatest friend. We found him charming; charming. We told him that he must often drop in, and he said he would. Now, Edmund, don't lose any time in thanking Miss Nash."

He was glad of an excuse for going; the more he thought about the things he had said to Fran Nash, the more deeply he

140

regretted them. He remembered that the school holidays were not far away; it would be a relief to wipe out the memory of a crushed piece of paper with an address written on it.

He drove to the house one evening after leaving office, and told Mr. Sefton that he was going.

"About time," Mr. Sefton said. "I was beginning to wonder if you had any reasons for keeping away. Had you?"

The question was an indication of the change that had come about in their relationship during the past weeks. Edmund could not have told how or when he had begun to like his godfather so much, but he knew that the sight of him propped on the edge of his desk, or lounging in the visitor's chair, was no longer unwelcome. The sarcastic remarks no longer irritated him, and he could meet the small, keen eyes with the knowledge that behind them was deep affection for him.

He evaded the question.

"I want to go and say thank you for my two Jamaicans," he said.

"That's only one of the things you should be grateful for," Mr. Sefton told him. "I don't know where I got the idea, but I'm beginning to think it must have been Fran Nash who talked you into letting Louisa and Freddie have that flat. Did she?"

"No, she didn't talk me into it."

"There's a gap somewhere," mused Mr. Sefton. "If I keep probing, I might be able to fill it—in time. Well, give them all my love."

"I will."

Campden Heights was not unfamiliar ground. The row of large, widely-spaced houses had long ago lost their wealthy tenants; most of them had been turned into flats. Edmund and his father had once considered buying one and selling it after conversion; the scheme came to nothing, but as he drove up the steep approach to the Heights, he recognised the house that he and his father had surveyed.

Number 11 was by far the shabbiest house in the street; its paint was peeling and its approach wild and overgrown. He stopped the car before the gate, and walked up to the front door wishing that he had telephoned to ask whether he might come. He had picked up the receiver and had put it down again, being unable to think of anything to say.

He rang the bell. Teck answered the door, and training enabled him to conceal his surprise and show only his pleasure. He led Edmund across a large, sparsely-furnished hall and into a very large, cold drawing-room which a small coal fire entirely failed to heat. Teck had not asked him to remove his overcoat, and the reason now became clear.

"I should take this chair, sir," he said. "It's got a high back and it keeps out draughts. To get this room really hot, sir," he added after a moment's hesitation, "requires a large fire constantly kept up. In the old days that used to be possible, but coal wasn't the price then that it is now. Miss Nash won't be long, sir."

"How is she, Teck?" Edmund enquired. "And how are the

children?"

"They're all well, thank you, sir. I hope Mr. and Mrs. Grand are proving satisfactory?"

Being assured that they were, he withdrew quietly and closed the door. Edmund, seated as near as possible to the fire, heard the front door opened and banged two or three times, but nobody came into the room and he assumed that the sounds had been made by the boarders. Then he was brought to his feet by the sound of a whistle.

He heard Teck hurrying to the front door, and guessed that Fran's arms were too full of parcels to allow her to use her key. She was still handing packages to Teck when she threw open the drawing-room door.

"I saw your car outside," she said. "You want a room? I'm full."

He smiled. He was so glad to see her that the room no longer seemed cold.

"I came," he said, "to thank you for Welty and Euphonia."

Teck closed the door; they were alone. She dropped on her knees by the fire and held her hands to the warmth.

"It was one way of getting you here," she said over her shoulder. "If you've finished saying thank you, I'd like to say I'm sorry. Sorry, I mean, for having shouted at you. I'm not sorry about the other things. Mr. Sefton says that Louisa and Frederica are as happy as sandboys—sandgirls—and he also said that he was glad you weren't engaged to Angela Wilde any more. That made me feel a bit better, but"—she twisted round to stare up at him—"if you're unhappy about her...is everything over for good?"

"There's a sort of impasse," he said.

"You mean it's a case of who'll make the first move?"

"I suppose so."

"Well, I couldn't get you another fiancée," she said, "but I could and did get you servants. Will you stay to dinner?"

"I...look, I came entirely without notice," he said. "I meant to ring up, but—"

"Vegetable soup, fried fish and baked apples. You could ring up your house and say you were going to be out."

He went into the hall and telephoned; when he came back into the room, she was still sitting on the hearthrug.

"Was your uncle glad to get the telegram?" she asked.

Edmund sat down.

"He thought I had a touch of the sun—but he wouldn't risk waiting until I came home, to find out for certain."

"You mean he was glad to get rid of them?"

"Very glad indeed."

She turned to look at him with a puzzled frown.

"You sound...different about him," she said. "Isn't he as nice as you thought he was?"

"Not quite."

He knew that she was waiting for him to enlarge upon his

bald statement; then she smiled.

"Before you get really warmed up to long speeches," she said, "I've learned that you have to be blazing angry."

"I'm not a very good talker," he said.

"Why not?"

He hesitated, choosing his words.

"I think," he said slowly at last, "my father made me believe what he himself believed—that everybody talks far too much. He told me that a question should be clear, and an answer concise, with no extraneous details offered to the questioner, who probably doesn't want them. He thought that men, sensible men, ought to choose their words with care and stick closely to the point. Women, of course, couldn't be expected to do anything of the sort."

And so confidences, enthusiastic descriptions and warm comments, he remembered, had been cut to a minimum as he had first admired and then emulated his father's admirable clarity and brevity of speech.

"Perhaps your reserve, or reticence or whatever it is, is one of the things I like so much about you," said Fran. "But if your father'd lived in this house, he wouldn't have changed his mind about everybody talking too much. They say that the only thing people can do nowadays is to sit and stare at Television every night—but in this house, everybody prefers to give their own performances. Does your uncle know that Angela gave you your ring back?"

"Yes, he knows."

"Is he trying to get you together again?"

He hesitated, and then realised that he had no desire to keep anything to himself.

"Angela," he said, "asked him to get in touch with me."

Her hands dropped to her lap, and her eyes searched his. "You mean she's trying to patch things up? Don't answer that; it isn't my business, and one of these days perhaps I'll learn what my own business really is—and learn to mind it. But when I knew that Mr. Sefton was your godfather, I talked to him about you. I asked him if he knew her, and he said he did, and he said that in his opinion, you're well out of it—which is what I thought before he said so, but it made me feel better. I suppose you think Mr. Sefton and I shouldn't talk about you behind your back, but we do. I like him. I—" She broke off, looked at the clock and rose to her feet with a cry of dismay. "Dinner! Could you bear to come into the kitchen and watch me cook it?"

"If I'll be in your way—" he began.

But she was on her way to the door. Following her, he saw it opening; on the threshold was a short, dark woman of about thirty and a very tall, very fair, very lean young man of about twenty-five.

"Mademoiselle Leonie Rimbault, Mr. Edmund Forth, Mr. Ivor Breck," said Fran rapidly as she crossed the hall. "Don't stop me; I've got to cook the dinner."

Mademoiselle Rimbault was dressed for the street, in a plain but well-cut black coat and high-heeled black shoes; the only touch of colour came from two little life-like robins perched on the brim of her black hat. She acknowledged the introduction with a slight bow, and addressed Edmund in grammatical but rather laboured and unmusical English.

"Please will you tell Fran, since you are going to follow her to the kitchen, that I have arranged another pupil for Ramon?"

"Why can't I tell her?" asked Mr. Breck lazily.

"Because I do not trust you, Ivor, to deliver messages correctly. Always you corrupt them. Sometimes this is a joke, sometimes it is not."

"Ramon doesn't get any extra money for these pupils you dig up for him," Ivor pointed out.

"He perhaps does not—but all the same, the school knows that they are there because of him, and this is a good thing. Now I must go."

"Why don't you take a day off now and then?" Ivor asked her.

"You know quite well why. When the restaurant is going well and my father is satisfied, I shall be satisfied too. At present, I am not."

She went out, and Ivor looked at Edmund and raised his shoulders in an exaggerated shrug.

"The Norman peasant strain," he said. "I don't know why

there are so many jokes about Scotsmen and Jews, when the prize for penny-pinching ought to be awarded to families like the Rimbaults. A lifetime of toil—with all the profits ploughed back into the business."

"If the restaurant isn't going well—began Edmund.

"It's just not going as well as all the other restaurants Papa Rimbault and his sons are running in the provinces in France. Leonie feels she's letting the side down. If you're feeling benevolent, you could collect parties of your richer friends and dine and wine them there."

Edmund was looking at him with a frown.

"I think," he said slowly, "I've met you before. Wasn't it at—"

But Ivor had raised a hand.

"Doesn't matter where," he said. "Just forget where. All I try to do now is keep out of the way of anybody who can carry wicked tales back to my grandmother."

"But I don't know your grandmother."

"Mr. Sefton does. It was your firm that surveyed my ancestral home and advised her to sell it."

"The Countess of Dellstone?"

"Why the surprise? I don't look blue-blooded? Actually, the blue blood only flowed into the family when my dear Granny married a second time. She caught a peer, but he died without leaving her anything, and she had to fall back on what my grandfather'd left her. She hung on to it while my parents were alive and she's still hanging on to it. She doles out a meagre allowance to me and she's waiting for me to pass my Law exams. She'll wait a long time."

He was leaning against the front door, which he had opened and closed for Mademoiselle Rimbault. Edmund would have given much for his easy, relaxed manner. He was dressed in drainpipe trousers, a loose sweater and a shabby leather jacket, and his expression was one of indolent amusement.

"But surely," Edmund said, "some of your friends—"

"They don't go down Tooting way," explained Ivor. "When I had this brilliant idea of chucking the exams and getting a job, I went after something in Soho. I haven't got brains, but I'm strong; can lift. Something about barrels of potatoes and pyramids of fruit has always fascinated me, and I enjoy handling them—but Soho, I found, was too tricky; all these new society cooks shop there. I moved out into the purlieus and got a job in a big fruit and vegetable concern, and the salary, plus dear Granny's allowance, will keep me alive until dear Grannie's dead. But if she gets wind of how I live, she'll cut me off. Fantastic, isn't it, that she can leave what's mine to anybody or anything she fancies?—This place of yours in Portugal sounds rather attractive. We get all the details from the kids when they're home. Regular Lusophiles." He straightened and led Edmund towards the kitchen. "Let's go and superintend, shall we?"

But before they had crossed the hall, a door at the end of a passage opened and an old man called to them in a high,

149

querulous voice.

"Fran back?"

"Yes," said Ivor. "Want anything?"

"Did she bring the record?"

Ivor picked up a flat package from the hall table.

"This looks like it," he said. "What is it?"

"None of your jazz," snarled the old man. "Bach's Mass in B Minor, if you want to know."

"I'll come and listen to it," said Ivor. "Oh—this is Mr. Forth, who owns that sizeable chunk of Portugal. Mr. Bisley."

Mr. Bisley opened his door a little wider, and Edmund saw that he was very small and thin, with white hair falling away from a balding and shrivelled pate. His hands were misshapen claws.

"How d'ye do. Don't know much about Portugal," he said. "Went there when I was young. Painted there. Forget the name of the place."

"Nazaré?"

"No."

"Sesimbra?"

"No, no, *no,*" Mr. Bisley said, in staccato irritation. "High. Bare. Lonely. Stark."

Something stirred in Edmund's memory. A faint suggestion came—and went. There was nothing definite, but he was left with a feeling that something, someone from the past had nudged him—and left without vouchsafing any explanation.

Ivor, with a nod to him, took the record from the table and followed Mr. Bisley to his own part of the house, and Edmund was left to find his way to the kitchen.

He glanced round, taking in the details of the well-shaped hall and the beautiful curving staircase. The door of the dining-room was open, and he could see Teck laying the table; beyond was a smaller room in which could be seen an open Television screen and a collection of old and battered toy animals; there was a bookshelf filled with what Edmund guessed to be juvenile literature; clearly this was the room in which Kerry and Belinda, when home, spent their leisure.

He went into the kitchen and found Fran in a white overall, standing at the kitchen table dipping fillets of fish into egg and then bread-crumbing them.

"Sit on that stool," she said, "and talk to me."

"What about?"

"Montebarca. If the children were here, they'd want to know how Zefa is, to say nothing of Conceição, Laurinda, Gracinda, Isaura, Josefina, José, Bruno, Domingo, Duarte and Manuel. And Tia Maria-Jesus, and did the lambs get born, and how many pigs altogether, and wasn't it true that those Ali Baba jars to keep vinegar in were over nine feet high, because nobody at school would believe it."

"When do they get back?"

"Twenty-third. What do you think of my boarders?"

"I like young Breck. But news of what he's doing must

get back to his grandmother eventually, mustn't it? Doesn't she ever come to London?"

"No. Ivor got her doctor to tell her she ought to stay put—so she does. Why don't you bring Louisa and Frederica to see me?"

"They'd like to come. They—"

He paused to listen; somebody on an upper floor was playing a guitar.

"Nice, hm?" said Fran after a time.

"I'm not musical, as I told you before," he said.

She looked at him in surprise.

"You don't have to be musical to know that that's guitar-playing of the very highest order. That's *playing* a guitar. Anybody can strum strum strum on one—but just listen to those lovely chords and trickly melodies."

He listened.

"It always sounds to me," he confessed at last, "as though somebody's playing a long introduction to a tune that never comes."

"You mean you don't like real Spanish music? Real Spanish dancing? Stamp stamp stamp?"

"Well...yes and no."

"You'll get a lot of it if you come to see us. Ramon brings his friends here and they dance—and sing. I suppose you don't like that kind of singing either?"

"Well. .. some of it sounds to me like a sound track of an

Eastern bazaar.—Can't I do anything to help you?"

"It's all ready, thanks." She glanced out of the window. "Look at that. Out there, sleet and fog. And at Montebarca, there's—"

"—rain and more rain. What did you do with the twenty-seven-pound car?"

"It's in the garage I bought it from; they're trying to replace those bits of string you saw with real pieces of engine. If they can make it go properly, I'll keep it and take the children on picnics next summer. Local picnics. They—" She raised her voice and shouted through the closed door. "No, Ramon. Go away!"

Castanets answered her, clicking appealingly, beseechingly, insistently.

"No!" she shouted. "You had tea, and dinner's practically ready."

Click, krr, krr, krrrr, Click.

"If I give you anything, I'll have to give it to Ivor too."

Krr, krr, krr.

"Oh—come in," she said impatiently.

She took some cheese out of a cupboard, cut a thick slice of bread and buttered it. The door had opened cautiously; a rather small, thin young man stood watching anxiously. He had black hair, a dark, craggy face and very large, very mournful eyes.

"There." Fran handed him the sandwich and he bit into it

with a smile of gratitude.

"Good, good," he said through an ample mouthful.

"This is Mr. Forth. Edmund, this is Ramon, who seems to need seven meals a day. Why did I think Spaniards lived on bread and garlic sausage?"

"In home," Ramon explained, "hot; here cold, hunger. Here"—he waved his free hand towards the dreary scene outside—"much..."

He looked expectantly at Edmund.

"Fog?" offered the latter.

"Yes. Fog. And much—" He sketched his need. "Rain?"

"No. Other. Brrrr."

"Snow?"

"*Si*. Snow. So in here"—he indicated his stomach—"empty. Need more .."

"Nourishment?"

"Please?"

"Food?"

"*Si*. Food. Breakfast early, much long to..."

"Lunch?"

"Yes. Need to eat. Tea very small, dinner long. I like to have.. ."

"Snacks in between?"

"Please?"

"The occasional sandwich?"

"The...?"

Edmund was getting tired; the effort of trying to find out what Ramon wanted to say, and saying it for him, was exhausting.

"You like to eat more often ?"

"*Si.* Yes," stated Ramon decisively. "Good .. ."

"Good food here?"

"No. Yes, yes, but have good..."

"Appetite?"

"*Si.* App-e-tite."

He finished his sandwich, wiped his mouth, leaned across the table, lifted Fran's hand gently and laid a light kiss upon it. Then he went out and the castanets were heard clicking jubilantly up the stairs.

"He does that to everybody—makes them find the words for him," Fran said. "Why should he learn English if he can get other people to speak it for him, is his idea. He's got a tragic sort of look, hasn't he? Very misleading. Belinda called him exotic, but she spelt it with two g's." She stopped and stared at him for some moments. "It seems odd," she said slowly, "to see you here. I thought..."

"You thought?"

"Well, I wondered if I ever would. Because in a way, I've messed up your life, haven't I?"

"You've changed it in a good many ways. In a good many ways, perhaps, it needed changing."

155

"Are you sure it really amuses you to sit on a stool and watch somebody cooking dinner?"

"Yes, I'm sure."

"In that case—"

She broke off abruptly. The front door had banged with a violence that shook the house, and from the echoes there came a sound that brought Edmund to his feet and chilled his blood—long, high-pitched, half scream, half war-cry, repeated again and again and again.

He looked at Fran. She was standing stock still, her eyes wide, her attitude one of tense expectancy.

"Oh *no*," she murmured under her breath. "Oh no, no, *no!*"

For a moment she seemed frozen—and then she had leapt to the door, turned back to seize Edmund's hand and was dragging him in her wake into the hall, into which the others were spilling: Ramon from upstairs, Teck from the dining room, Ivor from the Bisley's part of the house; Mr. Bisley himself and a large, comfortable-looking, good-humoured woman Edmund took to be his wife.

And by the front door, legs apart, arms flung high and wide, the call still coming from his lips, was the most outstandingly beautiful young male Edmund had ever seen. His body had the perfection of old Greek statues; his face and hair were dark, his eyes vividly blue and lashed like a woman's. Like Ivor, he was dressed in tight trousers and a leather jacket, but under the jacket was a brightly-coloured shirt. He was holding, for the benefit of his audience, the attitude of one transported with joy.

The hall was filled with sound—the yell from the man at the door, Ivor's questions, Fran's eager requests for an explanation, Mr. Bisley's irritated demands for silence.

Then Fran went up to the newcomer, took his face between her hands and kissed him warmly.

"You've got it!" she said. "Jonathon, you've got it!"

He swept her up into his arms and waltzed round the hall in ecstasy.

"I've got it! I've got it!" he chanted. "I'm made! I'm on the way! I'm—"

"Stop clowning," ordered Fran, "and put me down and talk sense."

He halted and put her on her feet, and there was an expectant silence; everybody waited for the story. But he was an actor, and he had an audience, and he was in no hurry.

"Yes, I've got it!" His voice had dropped to a deep- throated growl. His hand went through his hair and left it hanging over his forehead. He turned up the collar of his leather jacket and became a sinister and frightening figure. "I said to them: 'Give!' And I pulled a knife on them—see? And they—"

"Oh Jonathon, stop acting," wailed Fran in protest, "and *tell* us!"

He laughed and then spoke in his natural voice.

"I knew it was my part," he said. "From the first, I knew it. And they knew it too—but how d'you get on in this profession? I'll tell you how—you stand by and you watch the other fellows with strings pulling them. I knew that if they could only *see* me in the part... it'd be mine. And that's where Fran's idea came in."

"It worked?" she cried in wonder. "It really worked?"

"It really—" He stopped abruptly, his eyes on Edmund. "A stranger, listening to my secrets!" he declaimed. "A stranger decked in foreign attire—"

"Oh, get *on* with it!" implored Ivor. "That's Edmund Forth of Montebarca. What was this idea of Fran's?"

"To *pose* the part. Instead of hoofing it in and out of the agent's, she said, hoof it to the theatre in which they're rehearsing, and—"

"You mean they'd actually given someone else the part?" Ivor asked.

"Three other people. One after the other, naturally," Jonathon said. "One dropped out—no good, as I'd known he wouldn't be. Then the second. But the third seemed to be sticking it, and I got frightened. But Fran pointed out that what they wanted was a *picture*. This wasn't a speaking part: at least, there weren't more than a dozen lines to say. It was a picture of a man—a young man, a husky man, a good- looking-like-me man, and all he had to do in the play was to lean against a lamp-post and smoke—and that's all. But not quite all. There had to be *something*. There had to be enough to make the women look, and look again—and again. And that was where all the others went wrong. Because they'd seen screen stars doing just that—standing humped against something, looking sexy—and they all did faithful copies of the act. But I said to Fran: 'They're wrong, Fran; they're all wrong. You don't get famous by making the world say, or the agents say, or your fellow-actors say that you're exactly like so-and-so, the big star. That takes you half the way, but no more. To go the whole way, you've got to have something new, something exciting, something big. You haven't got to stand against a lamp-post trying to be like someone else. You've got to be *you.* You won't walk to the top in anybody's shoes but your own.'—And so I did it, Fran. I went to the theatre and I leaned against a lamp-post—like this."

He chose the hall stand, but anything else, Edmund thought, would have done as well. He was a young man on a street, listless, bored, leaning against the nearest support— but his eyes looked out at the world with a terrifying challenge. He was waiting—for what, nobody could guess, but nobody could be in any doubt that when it came, tragedy would come in its wake. He was an animal, with an animal's instinct to destroy.

Nobody spoke. When at last Jonathon stirred and became himself again, he looked round and smiled.

"See what I mean?" he said. "I did just that, and there was no copy-of-an-original about it. I was me—and terrific, and they all saw me as they went in. Yesterday. But I wasn't there when they came out. I was behind a lorry up the road, and I saw them looking—and talking. I knew what about. So today, I was there again—when they went in. I gave them exactly ten minutes. I prayed! I really prayed! Our Father, I said to myself...well, no, not to myself; Our Father, make those ruddy producers in there see straight, think straight for once. And they did. I saw old Hold-me-higher padding his—"

"Holby Prior?" breathed Fran.

"Didn't I say so? Himself. I dropped my cigarette, trod on it—contemptuously—and hitched up my pants, and I was on my way—he thought. 'One moment,' he says— peremptory-like. So I turned. I turned round and looked at him. Like this."

He surveyed them, in his bored gaze the look of a man who has seen a slug in his soup.

"What did he *say?*" asked Fran.

"He said: 'One moment'—again. But this time, the grit had gone out of it. I gave my pants another hitch and turned on my heel—and this time, he took two of those puttering little steps he does, and he put his hand—his fat, white fingers with the fat red rings—on my shoulder. And then I whirled and brother! did he two paces backwards, march! And I said to him—between my teeth—'Look, friend, if that's your lamp-post I was leaning on, you can have it, and you know what for, but you keep your mitts off me, see?' And as I was saying it, he looked like a man who'd been standing just under Heaven when the pennies began to fall. Would I step inside the theatre a moment? he said. I would not, I said. He had a proposition,

160

he said. Tell it to the cops, I told him. No, no, no, he said, all he was was a theatrical producer. *All!* Big joke—but I didn't laugh. I said: 'Fine, friend, fine, you just go on with what you were being and I'll go on with what I was doing, which was minding my own business.' And it took him all of fifteen minutes to get me to set foot inside and there they all were, except the guy they'd fired. 'This is what we want you to do,' they said—and there I was, surrounded by a bunch that must have added up to thirty thousand a week in salaries. 'Stand there and do what you were doing,' they said. So I did. The job was in my top left-hand pocket, and I knew it; all I had to do was to see that they knew it too. And I got it—the job. No talking— ten lines, but I'm on-stage so much that anybody in the audience who can't draw me by heart by the first interval will have to have his eyes examined."

"But a *contract,* Jonathon; a contract!" Fran said.

"I'm coming to that. Old Hold-me-higher ran through the first act and then he said we ought to tie it up; put it in writing. So I said that was all right with me, and I went with him to Pulson's and when we went in, Pulson looked at me and he was just going to say 'What, you here again, you?' when Hold-me-higher said, 'Steve, I want you to sign up a discovery of mine.' So we all signed, and Hold-me-higher went home and Pulson said, 'Why, you so-and-so, he'll soon find out you've been acting for years.' And I said, 'So he will, but he won't say much, because the joke'll be on him.'— And so I'm made. I'm as good as at the top. What makes stars faster than getting one good part that's *them*? Nothing. And now we can all go in and drink to me. Fran, where's that wine you got from Portugal?"

The wine was brought; Edmund, as the grower and donor, was toasted—and then they stood round Jonathon and drank to his future. Dinner was a celebration; when Edmund at last left the house, he was accompanied to his car by Fran, Ivor, Jonathon and Ramon, and sped on his way by the sound of a guitar.

He drove slowly, his emotions divided almost equally between happiness and confusion. When he reached his house, he felt disinclined to go in, and was glad to see a light in the flat. Putting his car away, he glanced at his watch: ten- thirty; perhaps it was not too late....

He went down the steps, and Louisa's head appeared at the window.

"It's *Edmund*! Come *in*!" she cried. "No, dear boy, of *course* it's not too late. Freddie dear, do open the door—it's Edmund. How nice, my dear boy, how nice of you to come in for a little chat. Sit there, Edmund; are you comfortable? Will you have a little of Freddie's ginger wine?"

He thanked her, but refused; he had tasted it once and did not care to taste it again.

"Don't you find it a little...strong?" he asked.

"Of *course* it's strong, dear boy. That's why it's so good! Freddie and I have a thimbleful at a time, with some nice little biscuits."

The flat was centrally heated, but the heating was not on. He made no comment, but was ashamed to realise that this was the first time he had ever wondered how much they had to live on, and whether they could afford to live at all. This was not the time to touch, delicately, on the subject, but it was one that they must soon discuss.

"Mr. Sefton popped in and had a little curry with us," Louisa said. "He says he's never tasted anything like it."

"You seem," he ventured, "to eat rather a lot of curry. Don't you perhaps get a little tired of it?"

"Tired of it?" Louisa exclaimed in astonishment. "But Edmund dear, it's so varied. And it's so *EconOMical.* You can put anything into a curry, dear boy; *ANY*thing! You don't have to use chicken or prawns except as a special treat. That nice curry we gave you on the Thursday before Welty and Euphonia came, that you said you enjoyed so much—do you know what that was? You thought it was delicious, and so it was, but I made it of all the little bits and pieces I'd been saving: a few beans that were over, some outside leaves of a cabbage—it's such a *waste* to throw them away, but they don't look well if you give them to people as they are. Little pieces of stale bread—that saves flour for thickening the gravy—and the bits of apple or pear that have gone a little too far: all that goes to make a delicious flavour, and how else could you use it all up except in curry? It's thrifty, it's nourishing, it's tasty; *that* is why we eat so much of it, or rather, have it so often."

No heating, and curried scraps. Curiosity began to stir in

163

him, and he studied them for the first time with genuine interest and affection.

"What exactly did you do out in India?" he asked.

"Well, my dear Edmund"—Louisa gave her extraordinary donkey-neigh, and he had to wait until her amusement subsided.—"That's a tall order for a little after-dinner chat! We were out there for forty-six years, you know. Doing useful work, I hope. I went out before Freddie. I was engaged to a tea-planter, and he was to have come to meet the boat at Bombay and we were to have been married. But at the last moment, something—I shall never know what—came over me. It—speak up, Freddie dear."

"A premonition," breathed Frederica.

"Perhaps," agreed Louisa. "But quite suddenly one day, in the middle of buying some things for my trousseau, I turned and said to Freddie: 'Freddie, you've got to come out with me to India.' Well, Freddie refused to come *with* me, but she said she'd come *after* me. She'd let me get the marriage over and done with and give me a little time to settle down on the tea garden, and then she'd come out. My fiancé had often suggested it, you know; a tea-garden is a lonely place for a woman, and he always thought it would be a good thing to take Freddie out. So that was how we arranged it, and I went out, and I stood on the deck and looked and looked."

She paused and looked at her sister; Frederica's hands were spread in a gesture denoting emptiness.

"Quite so," said Louisa. "Nobody. He wasn't there. I'd
164

come thousands of miles—for nothing. He had simply lost his courage at the last moment, and failed to come. And *that*, my dear Edmund, is why I became something of a family joke. Engagements are made and broken these days and nobody thinks anything of it, but at the time I'm speaking of, a girl in my situation was called jilted, and her situation aroused as much amusement as indignation. But what Frederica and I have never told anybody, simply because we knew they wouldn't have believed it, was that my only feeling was one of *stuPENdous* relief. Nothing more. Later, I will admit to feeling a little angry, not at what he had done, but at the manner of the doing— but my first reaction was relief. I knew that I myself had been losing my courage—and *that* was why I had begged Freddie to come with me."

"And then?" Edmund asked.

"Then? I was in Bombay and I was jilted. People tried to be kind, but all of them, on landing, had to hurry away to various parts of India. I wasn't by any means destitute; Freddie and I had our nice comfortable little incomes, and they went a long way in those days. So I found a small hotel and I waited for Freddie; I didn't tell her what had happened, because I had fallen in love with India and I wanted to stay there. When Freddie arrived, we had a little talk, and we decided to open our little school for Indian children. We —yes, Freddie dear?"

"Free, of course," Freddie said.

"Of course. People laughed a great deal—Edmund, have you ever heard the proverb: Fools laugh at what they do not understand? It's a very *true* one. But we opened our little school and after a time we got some children and then some more, and we taught them handicrafts and taught them how to be clean. The Church people came to us and thought we should teach them religion, but we didn't feel qualified to do that. We asked an English chemist to make us up little boiled sweets with a drop of cod liver oil inside—that was when vitamins came into fashion—and you can't *think*, dear boy, what a difference it made to those little mites. The only mistake we made in the end was in not realising how out of touch we were with England and with English ways and—yes, Freddie dear?"

"English people," Freddie said.

There was a pause; Louisa, for once, seemed to be hesitating.

"Don't think for a moment, Edmund dear," she said at last, "that Freddie and I don't appreciate what your Uncle Robert tried to do for us. All I'm saying is that perhaps he did it in the wrong way. When you're asking anybody to put people up, dear boy, it isn't wise to let it be known in advance that they're odd. Especially if they're not odd. Perhaps Freddie and I have our odd little ways, but I cannot think that Robert was justified in telling our relations that we were eccentric and .. . well, impossible. I think we could have been very happy with, for instance, poor little lonely Ella Forth up in Whitby, or dear old Millicent Forth in Cheshire, but by that time we had acquired a reputation for .. . well, dear boy, your Uncle Robert had really made us into a *joke*, and not a kind joke. As I've so often said to Freddie, we would have shown better sense if we'd accepted Walter's offer and—"

She stopped abruptly, halted by a warning hiss from Frederica.

"We had got out of *touch,*" she went on hastily, "and we—"

"Just a moment," said Edmund.

She looked stricken, but she answered his questions frankly.

"You said," he began, "that Walter—Walter Forth?"

"Yes, Edmund."

"Walter Forth made you an offer. He didn't," he said slowly, "offer you Montebarca, by any chance?"

"We didn't *want* it, Edmund dear. At least, we thought that, lovely as it was, we ought to come *home*. Never for one moment, in all those forty-six years, did Freddie or I ever want anything else but to die at home in England. But—"

"You *know* Montebarca?" he broke in in astonishment. "You've *been* there?"

"Many, many, *many* years ago, Edmund dear. You see... well, Walter was very close to us, you know."

"No, I didn't know. I don't know anything about him except the fact that he stayed with us when I was twelve, and left Montebarca to me when I was twenty-six."

"Which was very sensible of him," said Louisa warmly. "There couldn't be anybody in the world who deserves it more than you."

"But... he'd offered it to you, and you refused it?"

"Yes," Louisa said. "You see, we'd known him all our lives. He was born in Portugal, but he was educated in England, and he used to spend his holidays with us and we got very fond of him. He wanted to—now Freddie dear, Edmund may as well know the whole truth—he was very much in love with Freddie, and he wanted to marry her. She refused him; not once but many times. When she went out to India to join me, I think he gave up hope, but he never forgot her."

"When did you see Montebarca?" he asked.

"Many years ago. He wrote and *begged us* to go there after hearing that we were going to pay a visit to England. So we said we would, and we did. And we were so happy that we put off coming to England, and then there was a war and we couldn't come home and had to go back to India. But we were so happy there, Edmund dear. What a beautiful place it is!"

They brought out a photograph album and showed him photographs of Walter Forth, and of Walter's father James. James was a lanky, sad-looking man with untidy grey hair and a straggling moustache—but as Louisa talked, he emerged as a vital young man who had gone out to Portugal from an English cork factory in the late eighteen hundreds and wandered through the cork districts of Portugal buying and shipping cork to his native country and laying the foundations of a flourishing trade. Edmund learned of the buying of Montebarca and numerous other properties, since sold; he heard of the dangerous early days, when thieves and brigands lay in ambush on the roads of the Alentejo waiting to spring out and seize cork loads from defenceless drivers. James Forth had put an end to that by organising convoys of oxen carts, two hundred and more, each driver armed with a rifle; the convoys set out from remote parts of the region and travelled slowly but safely to Montijo, whence the cork was shipped down the Tagus to Lisbon. The descendants of the armed drivers were still at Montebarca; the workers on the estate were the sons and grandsons of those who had served James and Walter Forth.

And the story to which he was listening, Edmund realised, could have been told by nobody but Louisa and Frederica. Nobody else knew so much of Walter, remembered so much about James.

"And about twelve years ago," Louisa ended, "Walter wrote and asked us if we would accept Montebarca and live the rest of our lives there. But we were old, Edmund dear, and we longed for England—always, always England—and we refused. And how well that we did! How wonderful that in the end, *you* should be the one to have it!"

They had refused Montebarca. And he, who had inherited it, had refused them a home, a refuge. ...

"We weren't going to tell you," he heard Louisa saying. "Freddie said that I must be careful, in case you should think that we regretted anything—which we don't in the least. So I was careful, but I must say, Edmund dear, that it's lovely to be able to stop being careful, and to talk about it freely at last. Is old Joaquim still alive?"

"No. His son's in charge. Tia Maria-Jesus is there."

"She's *still* alive?" roared Louisa in astonishment. "No! But if *we're* alive, why shouldn't *she* be? She wasn't very much older than we were. Oh Edmund, how beautiful it was! All those lovely soft colours and—speak up, Freddie dear... of *course*! Edmund, dear boy, you must have *seen*!"

"Seen?" he echoed.

"All Freddie's beautiful little water colours that she did while she was there—Walter framed them himself and hung them up and wouldn't let us bring them away because he loved them so. How *odd*, Edmund dear, that when you saw Freddie's pictures on these walls you failed to recognise her work."

Freddie's, he thought dazedly. So that was where he had seen the two-tone wish-wash before: on the Montebarca walls. Brown for the cork, for the workers, for the soil. Green for the vines and the olives and the orchard and the sky. Freddie's. He would have thrown them out—but Tia Maria-Jesus had known better than he what they represented.

It had been the only change he made. That—and nothing more.

All he had done was remove Walter Forth's memories of his cousin and lifelong love, Frederica.

Chapter Nine

"Miss Wilde," Miss Brady said, "left a message just before you came in this morning, Mr. Forth: will you please meet her for lunch at the Welton at one fifteen."

He merely nodded, but the words sounded like an echo from a distant, forgotten past. How long, he wondered, was it since his Uncle Robert had gone storming down St. James's to report that his nephew had lost his mind? One month? Two? How long was it since he had thought of Angela—except fleetingly . ...

And now—lunch at the Welton, as so often before. She would come in wearing a suit that would screw all the other women's heads round as though they'd been attached to a single string. She would be hatless, and her blonde, beautiful head would pick up men's eyes as it passed, and hold them. She would be quite unselfconscious as she came through the tables to join him—she refused to meet in the bar. She would look casual, and rather bored—until she smiled at him—and the waiters wouldn't mind how long she took over her choice of a meal, because although light, it would be a very, very expensive meal indeed. She would sip a little white wine, smoke a cigarette with her coffee and make up her lips before leaving, and he would be aware throughout the meal that there wasn't a woman in the place to touch her, or a man who didn't wish he could. The women would be jealous of her, and the men would be jealous of him. And he ...

His musing came to an end; Mr. Sefton had come in with the leisurely air he wore whenever he had gossip to impart.

"Ran across your Uncle Robert yesterday," he said. "Did you know he was going into politics?"

"Yes."

"He'll end up in the Cabinet; see if he doesn't. Unless something trips him up. Wish it could be me."

Edmund laughed, and hearing himself laugh, marvelled at the changes that had lately taken place in his life. They had brought him a great deal of happiness—but nothing, perhaps, gave him more satisfaction than the affectionate relationship which now existed between his godfather and himself. They met frequently outside the office—at Edmund's house, or down in the flat, where Mr. Sefton was a constant visitor; curry, he said, had become his staple diet. They met at Campden Heights and when they left, left together and went to Mr. Sefton's three tidy little rooms and sat by the electric fire and talked far into the night. He found the old man not only amusing, but wise, informative and well-read. He also found him willing to talk continually about Fran Nash and her family of boarders. They discussed Ivor's grandmother, Leonie's restaurant and Ramon's hopes of joining a Spanish dance company that was shortly coming to England. They walked across to sit in the Bisleys' rooms, and played chess with the old man. They seldom spoke of Fran herself, but with her Edmund was on terms which after long deliberation he described to himself as brotherly.

"I'm lunching with Angela today," he told his godfather.

The old man's eyes narrowed.

"And why?" he asked.

"Because she asked me to."

"At her house?"

"At the Welton."

"Ah." Mr. Sefton relaxed. "Public meeting. That's safe enough."

Edmund looked across the desk and spoke slowly.

"You never liked her, did you?" he asked.

"Never. If you'd asked me before you burnt your bridges, I would've told you so. But not later. And anyway, in that not-so-far-off time, you weren't much interested in my opinions."

"Why not later?"

"Why not? There's a time to be frank and a time not to be, that's why. If I had a wife, and if she bought a hat and put it on and said 'George dear, how do I look?' I wouldn't tell her until I'd ascertained whether she'd actually paid for the hat or whether she had it out on what's called approval. If she'd paid for it, and if there wasn't any chance of her getting the money back, 'Quite nice, dear' I'd say. But if she hadn't paid for it,

I'd tell her the truth and urge her to hurry back to the shop and report the saleswoman who'd told her it suited her. You follow me?"

"So far, yes."

"Well, the same goes for Miss Wilde. You were engaged: fine. I, as your godfather, am told the news—and learn that it is official. So I say 'My blessings, m'boy.' If you hadn't been such an unapproachable chap, I'd have pressed a small cheque into your hand—but you didn't encourage friendly acts, my dear Edmund. However, this is a friendly act I'm doing now. I'm advising you to leave the beautiful Miss Wilde exactly where she is now: nicely planted on the horns of her little dilemma."

"I don't—"

"—see the dilemma? You ought to. Most men of your intelligence would—but if a man was born with a blind eye, you're him. He. From the time you were *so* high, you've seen what you wanted to see—and nothing more. Shall I elaborate?"

"This is the middle of a rather busy morning," Edmund pointed out.

"True. But more important than the firm of Forth is Forth's happiness. And that's what you're risking. You're like a small boy who put out his hand to touch a red-hot poker—but somebody whisked it away in time. Now he's trying to touch it again. The only thing that's wrong with that metaphor is that Miss Wilde doesn't resemble, even remotely, a red-hot poker. If she got anywhere near a red-hot poker, it would give a spit and a fizzle—and go stone-cold."

"Are you trying to tell me I shouldn't—"

"Obey this summons? No. I'm only asking you to go to this lunch in blinkers so as not to be melted by her undeniably good looks. Go with your eyes shut and your mind wide open. I knew her mother when she was a young woman, and a bigger bitch never gave birth to a littler bitch. They're poison, both of them, Edmund. I couldn't say any of this while you were engaged to her, but I can say it now. If you marry Angy Wilde, you'll live to regret it. Any questions?"

"Yes. What's her dilemma?"

"She talked herself, in a fit of temper, into a very, very difficult position. She made it almost impossible for you to get in touch with her, which means that she's had to be the one to climb down. She wouldn't have done that unless she'd wanted something very, very badly. And what she wants very badly is you."

Edmund smiled. "Did you ever advise my father about his love affairs?"

"No. It's no-man's-land. All I'm doing now is trying to lead you a little bit farther away from the precipice. Angy's a very clever woman and she nearly always gets what she goes after. If you marry her, it'll be the finish of me in the firm: you cannot call the boss's wife a bitch and live to get promotion. But then I never wanted promotion, and your father knew it; that's why you're sitting in that chair and I'm sitting in this

175

one. I worked to get my bread and butter and a bit of jam, and when I got them, I relaxed. I tried to get your father to relax too, but he wouldn't—and that's why I'm here now instead of him, to enjoy watching his son turning into a warm-blooded man at last. One of these days, I'd like to know what made you send that extremely out-of-character telegram to your uncle."

"One of these days, you shall."

"And in the meantime, take a good long look at Angela Wilde and make an effort to see what's under that alabaster skin. Do you want to marry her?"

There was a very long silence. After a time, Mr. Sefton got up and walked to the door and opened it.

"I'm glad," he said, before going out. "Good luck."

At his table in the Welton, Edmund knew as he watched Angela walking towards him, that all the pointers indicated that the luck was already his.

He had risen, and she was smiling—not the smile he had been used to seeing, but one half quizzical: where, she seemed to be asking, had the calm, sensible, intelligent Edmund gone?

He was asking himself the same thing. Where was the man who had once, after her entrance, had difficulty in taking his eyes off her and focusing them on the menu? Where was the pride that had flowed through him as she took her place at his table? Where was the pleasure of listening to her as she discussed, crisply and sensibly, their future?

His mother and his nurse, he remembered suddenly, had

had a way of indicating disapproval when he was behaving badly. "Where's Edmund?" his mother would ask. "He's gone out, Madam," the reply had always been. "He's gone out and left a silly donkey in his place."

Certainly a part of him had gone out. He still thought her lovely. His eyes took in her beauty, his ears marked her musical voice, his senses registered her magnetism—but his mind was calm and wary and wide-awake. If a part of him had gone out, Madam, there was nothing silly about whatever had taken its place.

Her first words were spoken in a low and teasing voice.

"Darling Edmund, what's come *over* you? You're giving me such a lot of trouble! Am I never going to hear from you again?"

"You put up a difficult fence," he said.

"I know. But I was angry. Wouldn't you have been?"

"Yes. I would."

There was a pause; there was ordering to be done, the waiter's advice to be taken or rejected, sherry to be brought and poured and placed before them.

"Now," she said at last. "Explain why you didn't consult me before sending that telegram."

"I forgot to answer my uncle's letter. He sent a telegram and the answer had to be sent at once."

"Then your uncle was right; you must have had a touch of the sun, or a go of amnesia, or something. I would have said

177

I was entitled to at least as much consideration as a couple of old women you'd never set eyes on in your life, but I don't suppose this is the last difficulty from which I shall have to extricate you. They're in. The question now is how to get them out."

"There isn't a question," he heard himself saying.

The temperature, he thought, must have dropped twenty degrees. Her eyes were suddenly cold.

"I don't quite understand," she said.

"It's quite simple. If you remember, before leaving for Portugal I told you—at the last moment—that I'd been asked by my uncle to have Louisa and Frederica to stay with me. You and I gave the matter exactly three minutes—not long when you consider that we were discussing the future of two home-less people. We made a bad decision and—"

"We made a perfectly sensible decision. Then, in one of those holiday moods that seem to come over people some-times, you had a ridiculous impulse and you gave way to it. And now you're stuck with them. Why don't you admit it? Why all this highmindedness about homeless people?"

"I like Louisa and Frederica," he said, and heard her laugh.

"*Like?* Really, Edmund, you're going too far! In a mo-ment, I shall think you're really out of your mind. *Like* them! Have you forgotten that I *saw* them? Didn't my mother tell you that I'd been subjected to a whole chapter of insults? Do you know that they called my engagement ring —*your* ring— flashy?"

"It was flashy. I told you so at the time, but not emphatically enough," he said—and almost lifted a corner of the tablecloth and peered under the table to see where the voice had come from. His? That flat, authoritative, unanswerable tone?

He ought to do something—fast. She looked as though she was about to leave, and although he had no wish to keep her, he felt it his duty to send her back to her work reasonably well-fed. It was some time before she spoke, and when she did there was no longer any softness in her voice.

"Let me get this straight," she said. "Every time you have softening of the brain, am I expected to smile and swallow the consequences of whatever it is you've done?"

"All I've done," he pointed out, "is give two homeless old ladies a home. Let me admit that when I came home from Portugal and found them so deeply dug in, I had a feeling it would be hard to get them out. Then I found, to my surprise, that I liked them. They are, after all, my own flesh and blood. I like them and I am glad to have given them a home in which they're happy."

"Very well. They're happy and in a home and you're glad. And now we come to the question of a time limit. Am I to understand that because you've come to love and honour those two old harridans, I've got to take them on for life? Is that what you call being rational?"

"Was there anything rational in letting me be interviewed
179

by your mother on my return from Portugal—and handed my ring by a maid?"

"Your telegram to your uncle—without a word to me of your change of mind—was insulting. Yes or no?"

"For that, I've apologised. The telegram, in a way, was a mistake."

"Oh? Thank you for going so far, at last. If it was a mistake, it can be put right."

"Not," he heard the silly donkey saying, "by turning Louisa and Frederica out. They're there—to stay."

He saw her make a strong effort to control her temper. "Let me get this quite clear," she said. "You refuse to ask your cousins to leave?"

"I'm afraid I do."

"Very well. I'll offer you one last alternative. I'll agree to your paying the rent of some other flat for them—a reasonable rent for a flat in an entirely different district of London. I won't have them in my house, but if you want to go and see them and indulge this affection that's sprung up so suddenly, I've no objection to your doing so. But they insulted me, and that I won't forgive."

She had risen, brushing aside the waiter's questions about fruit and coffee. Edmund, standing and facing her, saw that she was white with fury, and suddenly found himself sorry for her. She was issuing ultimatums, and they were proving entirely ineffective. It was not a situation in which she often found herself.

But he, he reflected, had had to learn several lessons in the past few weeks, and perhaps there were one or two in the book she hadn't got quite right. He was, by her standards, or perhaps by any standards, in the wrong; she didn't know the full story and she never would, but she had a case; he had, so far as she knew, acted high-handedly if not actually insultingly; she had every right to be angry.

But her way out was no way out. Her last suggestion might appear to her to be reasonableness itself—but he would not agree to it.

"I'll give you a week to think about it," she said.

"I don't need a week. I don't need a day," he said. "I'm sorry, but I can't do it."

There was a short, very short pause.

"Very well," she said. "Then you can stay out of my life. Goodbye."

She was going—swiftly, and without looking back.

She had gone, and he did not think that she would come back, and with a sick feeling worse than anything he had ever experienced he knew that he did not in the least care.

Chapter Ten

The unfinished lunch at the Welton drew a clear line between Edmund's past and future. The past had gone, the future was uncertain.

The present was Campden Heights. He went there three or four times a week, sometimes with, sometimes without Louisa and Frederica. They had the advantage of being free during the day, and could visit the house when he was in the office. Fran Nash was a frequent visitor to the flat, and Mr. Bisley, getting on well with both the old ladies, had taken to summoning a taxi, putting his wife and himself into it and dropping in to see them. He was said by Louisa to admire the water colours immensely.

It was a cold, wet winter. Welty and Euphonia built up cheerful log fires in the drawing-room at Chelsea, and Edmund left them to go and sit, sweater-clad, in the crowded drawing-room at Campden Heights. The Christmas holidays came, and Kerry and Belinda were added to the circle; Edmund went with the former for long walks through the City, and learnt a great many new facts about its history. He helped Belinda to make puppets and to draw up her Christmas present list. He and Fran were once admitted through Jonathon to a rehearsal of the play, and crept into the sheeted stalls and had the privilege of witnessing a stirring battle between the producer and the star. He and Mr. Sefton gave a joint Christmas Eve party at Chelsea, and with Louisa and Frederica spent Christmas Day with the Nashes. He took Fran to dinner at the Rimbault and the children to most of the Christmas plays. He played chess with Mr. Bisley and tiddlywinks with Ivor. He spent busy hours in the kitchen, the only one permitted to do so; he accepted food and provided wine. He met numerous Spaniards that Ramon brought to the house, and learned to sit through long evenings of hand-clapping, foot-stamping, guitar-strumming, castanet- clicking and singing of a kind he thought lamentably tuneless. He held skeins of wool for Mrs. Bisley and found her calm good-humour an interesting contrast to her husband's testiness and irritability. He heard from Teck stories of Fran's mother and father, and began to form a picture of the house that was very different from its present-day shabbiness. The old man, he had come to realise, was in truth a pillar of strength. Quiet, unobtrusive, he had thought for the comfort and well-being of every member of the household; he turned Ivor's cuffs, patched Kerry's trousers, polished Ramon's high-heeled boots, made hot drinks at all hours, gave advice when asked and small sums of money when unasked. His life was the life of the Nashes; he had no other.

The end of December brought Edmund's birthday, and he celebrated it by giving a dinner party at his house; Leonie was unable to be present; the children were in bed and Mrs. Bisley disliked late nights—but Mr. Bisley, Mr. Sefton, Jonathon and Ivor were present, as were Fran and Louisa and Frederica.

"This," Ivor said, when the ladies had left the dinner table, "is what I call hospitality. Edmund, if I'm a judge, this is wonderful Madeira."

"You're a judge," said Edmund. "Jonathon, how's the play going?"

"Fair. Only fair," Jonathon said. "What can you do to make the king's daughter understand how a king's daughter behaves? She's got the title role, but—"

"Title role? I thought it was called Apples of Gold," said Ivor.

" 'Apples of Gold for the king's daughter,' " said Jonathon. "Don't you ever read?"

"Why don't you give up this standing-still part," Mr. Sefton asked, "and sign the contract that fellow offered you?"

"Because I'd have to leave London, that's why, and leave London I won't," said Jonathon. "I'm staying here until I'm a big name. I've seen too many guys sign too many contracts too soon. Some of them went roaring over to Hollywood with a tin contract, and you'd think they'd gone sailing over the precipice with the Gadarene swine, for all you've ever heard of them since. I'm staying here."

"Why didn't you take the comedy part the agents offered you?" Ivor asked.

"Because if you're in a hurry to impress the critics, you have to keep it serious," said Jonathon. "They look down their noses at light stuff. That's why I wanted to be in this play. Nobody'll be able to understand what it's about, but it'll be what's called a *succès d'éstime*—and there'll be two half-columns explaining how great it would've been, if only."

"But the great comedians—" began Mr. Sefton.

"Oh—the great!" Jonathon, his chair pushed back from the table, his legs outstretched, twirled his glass by its delicate stem. "That's different. A comic's a comic until he gets to the top, and then suddenly he's a clown with tragic undercurrents. Heartbreak under the grin. That fellow Pagliacci started it and it still goes."

"What's the play about?" Mr. Bisley asked.

"Sex," Jonathon said. "What else?"

"Think it'll run for long?" Mr. Sefton enquired. Jonathon hunched his shoulders.

"Doubt it," he said. "You know how it is—you have fashions and you have phases, and the present phase is pretty raw. What they call realism. Audiences have developed strong stomachs, and they don't feel grown-up unless you feed them red meat. We're only giving them one rape, and that's off-stage. We'll just have to wait and see. If it comes off, it comes off."

"When's it coming on?" Ivor asked.

"February. Try-out in Manchester."

"Pity my grandmother couldn't have come down. She used to be a regular first-nighter. Used to sweep in with tiara and twinklers. Could you use the publicity?"

"You couldn't," Edmund reminded him. "I'd leave her up there if I were you. Ramon, I thought you were joining a company and appearing in a Spanish show round about now."

"No theatre," Ramon explained. "Hall, no good in hall."

"Which hall?" asked Mr. Sefton.

"Hall in Breexton."

"Brixton!" exclaimed Ivor in astonishment. "You're taking a crowd of Spanish dancers to *Brixton?*"

"First there, afterwards theatre," explained Ramon. "When beeg success, get theatre. If get theatre, not more in Brixton."

"The thing seems to be full of ifs and whens," Ivor commented. "Edmund, couldn't we get Welty and Euphonia in to sing some calypsos?"

They gathered round the piano in the drawing-room and Ivor played while Welty and Euphonia sang some calypsos that were familiar, some that were strange, and some that were parodies. Of these last, the one they all liked best was:

Oh, I left Jamaica on a big white boat

An' I came to England with no winter coat.

But I found a warm girl and I settled down

Till I left that girl in Campden Town.

"All together," directed Ivor. "One, two: I *left Ja-mai-ca* on a big white boat..."

Welty, flushed with success, was led away by Euphonia to do the washing up, and in the comparative peace, Louisa's voice was heard once more and Jonathon gave a group in the corner a free run-through of all the parts in the play. Mr. Bisley wandered round the room looking at the pictures with Edmund, and stopped in surprise before the van Willans.

"You've got one of those, have you?" he said. "Know what they're fetching?"

"Yes. Five figures."

"Your father bought it?"

"My mother."

"Then she knew a thing or two. It's a good bit of work."

"It's my favourite picture."

"Ah." The keen old eyes looked up into his. "And why?"

"Perhaps because every time I look at it, I see something new."

"Fine artist," commented Mr. Bisley. "Got any more of his pictures?"

"Unfortunately, no. I made a bid for the one they found the other day—did you read about it?"

"Yes. Dug it up in a junk shop somewhere."

"Your wife paints, doesn't she?" Edmund enquired.

"Off and on. Everybody paints today. New fashion.— Got to go, I'm afraid; told my wife I'd be home early. Will you phone for a taxi?"

"I'll take you home."

"No, no, *no*" said Mr. Bisley. "Can't leave y'r own party."

"They're all quite happy," Edmund pointed out. "I'll be back before they know I've gone."

Fran and Mr. Sefton, seated together on the sofa, had been watching him.

"You see what I mean?" she said. "It's this getting-into-the-background business again. He gives a wonderful party, gives us all a wonderful time, keeps an eye on everybody to see they're enjoying themselves—"

"Aren't those all the duties of a good host?" Mr. Sefton asked.

"Well, yes—but he doesn't behave like a host; he does it all as though he's a...an organiser. He gives me the feeling that he wants to come and join in, but feels he wouldn't add to the success if he did. He's so...so *detached.*"

"And that worries you?"

"Yes, it does. It's worried me ever since he began coming to my house. At first I thought that he was ..."

"Feeling his way?"

"Yes. We all do that, more or less, but once we're in, we know we're in. Why doesn't he know?"

"Because under that rather platform manner, he's shy."

"With us? Still?"

Mr. Sefton looked from her to Edmund, standing with Mr. Bisley before one of the pictures, and for once, felt a little out of his depth. He knew that Edmund was happy, and he knew why. But Edmund, like himself, was moving at a pace faster than that to which he had become accustomed. Edmund, like himself, was having difficulty in keeping his feet, or his head, in rapidly-shifting circumstances.

His eyes rested on Fran. She was one of the rare women, he thought, who could be looked at with pleasure at any moment of the day. In the morning, she shone; at night, she glowed. Her mind seemed as healthy as her beautiful young body.

"Why aren't you talking?" he heard her ask.

"Do people have to talk all the time?"

"No, but I asked you a question and you've been an awfully long time thinking of an answer."

"There isn't any answer. Edmund's made friends with you all. He likes you all—very much. But he feels a bit older than the younger members of the group. You can't deny that there's a certain difference between men of twenty- six and men of thirty-six. If there isn't, there ought to be. Edmund's never been as young as he could have been. His mother died at the wrong time."

"I don't suppose she could help that. What was wrong about it?"

"He'd just come down from Oxford, and he found his father a bit lost. He got into the habit of spending as much time with him as he could. His father shouldn't have allowed it—or perhaps accepted is the better word. I wanted to say so, but you can't say much to a man who's just lost his life's companion—not if she meant as much to him as Edmund's mother did. So what was more natural than that father and son should stick together? That's what they did: golf, shooting, fishing, travelling. They were good companions, and it was fine for the old man, but it wasn't so good for Edmund."

"Is that when he decided to go into the firm?"

"That's when, and that's why. Perhaps it was a good thing, because he's been a success—but in those two years or so when he was so close to his father, he lost touch with his own age group. When his father died, he was twenty- six—and that was when he inherited that place out in Portugal. He went out to take a look at it—and you know the rest."

She looked at him thoughtfully for a time.

"You like him very much, don't you?" she asked at last.

"Almost as much as you do," he said.

He wondered whether—or what—she would have replied, but she had seen Edmund coming towards them.

"I shan't be long," he told them. "I'm just running Mr. Bisley home."

"Told him it wasn't necessary," grunted Mr. Bisley.

Fran got to her feet.

"I'm coming too—to keep you company on the way home," she told Edmund.

They were out of the door before anybody had realised

they were going. Ivor looked at Mr. Sefton with eyebrows raised.

"If any other girl said that," he commented, "you'd know exactly what she meant. With Fran, all you know is that she doesn't."

Edmund, having left Mr. Bisley at Campden Heights, drove back with Fran in silence. It was a long time since he had been alone with her, he mused; the boarders in the drawing-room, Teck in the kitchen...

He enjoyed, as he always did in winter, the contrast between the wet, cold, brightly-lit streets and the warm, dark interior of the car; he felt that he was in a little ship, sailing over the reflections of a busy harbour. The cafés were waterfront cafés, the blocks of flats brilliantly-lit liners. A barber's pole changed the picture and made it one of Venice, with painted poles leaning outward, waiting to pinion dark, noiseless gondolas.

"What," Fran asked at last, "are you thinking about?"

"Wet streets."

"All that time?"

"Yes. And you?"

"I was thinking about you. I was wondering whether you ever had any regrets—about *her.*"

"Angela? No."

"Mr Sefton thinks she wants you back. Do you want her back?"

"I think I prefer to let things remain as they are."

She drew a deep breath.

"It would have been awful," she said, "if it *hadn't* worked out."

"But you knew, of course, that it would?"

"I practically knew. It all depended on what kind of person you were—that was all I had to judge. If I thought you could have thrown Louisa and Frederica out after offering them a home, I might have been afraid to do it. But I was sure you couldn't, and wouldn't."

"And if I had been, finding them in the flat would have served me right?"

"Yes. Did you know that your uncle had called at the flat?"

Fear touched him.

"When?"

"Yesterday. But you needn't worry. Their front door's always locked and they never open it without looking out of the window first. Louisa looked out and saw him and said she was sorry but Freddie wasn't feeling up to visitors, and would he go away and come back in the Spring."

"And?"

"He was angry, of course. He said something about owing him some gratitude. So she shut the window, because she told me they didn't owe him anything. Where," she asked, "did you pick up the idea that your uncle was a kind man?"

"You form your estimates of uncles," he said, "when

192

you're rather young. Uncle Robert was good-looking and hearty—not too hearty—and tipped well and always looked the kind of man you wouldn't mind growing up to be."

"Your father didn't—"

"—tell me there might be another side to Robert? No. He must have known there was; he never went out of his way to see him. When he died, Robert began this head-of-the- family business, and it was in that capacity that he took up Louisa and Frederica. They became the family joke, and I'm sorry to say I thought it as funny as everybody else. What do you think he wants with them now?"

"Mr. Sefton thinks he's trying to get at them to tell them they're coming between you and your fiancée."

"But they thought her—"

"—a *creature*; yes. But if they thought you loved her, they'd start packing. So I forestalled your Uncle Robert."

"And how did you do that?"

"By telling them tonight, when we went upstairs after dinner, that he had pushed this girl at you and was still trying to do it. He is, too. I told them you didn't want her—so it's nice to learn that you don't. So you see I've been wielding my toy sword again.—Your uncle's trying to get into Parliament, isn't he?"

"I think that's the idea."

"And Angela would be pretty useful to have in the family?"

"Yes."

"Well, for Louisa and Frederica's sake, as well as for your own, keep her out of it. You're so calm about the whole thing that I don't think you know your own danger. Uncle Robert wants her in the family, and she wants to be in it, and—"

"I don't think she does. She has plenty of other offers she can take up."

"But what you don't understand is that they're not from *you*." She made an impatient movement. "I hate men who've got a high opinion of themselves, but you do go a bit too far in the other direction, it seems to me. What you don't seem to know is that a girl can have lots of men after her. If I'd wanted to get married, I could have done. Then why didn't I? If you want to know, I'll tell you. I'll tell you even if you don't want to know. It's because good things have a way of getting split up—they come in dribs and drabs. It took me twenty minutes to explain dribs and drabs to Ramon. For example: one man's wonderful to look at, but all he can do is talk about his travels, or his money, or his coloured slides. Well, it's nice to hear about travels and money and I like looking at coloured slides, but not when there's this 'I' stuck in the foreground. A man might be attractive, but there's something about the way he walks, or talks, or eats that in some way puts you off. Perhaps he's rich—but mean. He might be amusing at parties, but terribly dull the rest of the time. What I'm trying to say is that there's always a snag —*until.*"

"Until what?"

"Until suddenly you find someone with everything you want—and it's funny that it needn't be nearly as much as you thought you wanted. Suddenly there's everything. You had everything—for Angela. Love didn't come into it because she thought other things more important. You were more than presentable, you had more than enough money—and you had brains. Why do you think you had to be grateful when she said she'd marry you? You're not a man who has to get down on his knees in front of any girl; you can stand up straight and put a straight proposition and let her do the kneeling when next she says her prayers. What you've got to do is to weigh up all you've got to offer, because if you don't, you're just going to be ready for the next woman who has the sense to make a grab at you, and I don't want that. I want to—"

"Why not?"

"All I want is . ... What did you say?"

"Why don't you want that?"

"Want what? Oh, the next woman making a grab? Because I don't want to see you a victim, that's why."

"Why not?"

"Why not? That's a silly question. Because I like you, of course. We all like you—the children and the boarders and Teck. And Mr. Sefton. And Louisa and Frederica. And Welty and Euphonia. We don't want to see you grabbed; we want to see you in there, grabbing. We want—Look, you missed the turning."

195

"You noticed this time?"

"You mean you missed it before?"

"I've been going round the square for the past ten minutes. This is the tenth round."

"You can't go round a square. Why are we doing it?"

"Because getting back to Chelsea meant getting back to the others, and I wanted you to go on talking."

"Don't you get enough of that without going round squares?"

"I'm not often the only listener. I'm sorry you mentioned the toy sword."

"You've been doing a bit of toy-swording yourself," she told him gloomily. "You've gone and made me feel uneducated. Can you explain that? I never felt uneducated before I met you. Now I find myself sneaking in on the school Television stuff and trying to find out what the earth goes round, and why, and whether the planets circle the sputniks, or the other way round, if at all. And so on. It's very confusing—learning, and wanting to learn, both. I was taught it all at school, I suppose—all but the sputnik part— but it didn't seem important then, and now suddenly it does. There was a lesson on engines—car engines. Every girl and boy, the man said, ought to know the principles of the combustion engine—and I didn't even know that that car I bought had a combustion engine. Veins and arteries; I never could bear to look at those gory charts at school; I used to shut my eyes and feel grateful to God for covering us all up nicely—but now...If I'm ever to have children, oughtn't I to know where their muscles are?"

"Aren't you taking on rather a lot at once?"

"You have to, if you're making up for lost time."

"I don't think," he said, "that any of your learning time was wasted. Perhaps you didn't follow the charts, but you learnt—"

"—about people? About hat shops? About how to start with money and end up without any? That isn't education—that's just life. Don't you realise that I don't know *anything*?"

"You really want to become an engineer-anatomist?"

"Not in the least. I felt much happier when I didn't want to know anything. Why do you think you've had this effect on me?"

"Most of us," he told her, "go through a phase of trying to do the things we didn't do when we had the chance. If you're going to keep the car, I would, if I were you, concentrate on the combustion engine course and let the rest go."

They were home. He stopped the car and they sat without moving.

"Well, you live here," she said at last. "And there's a party going on inside. If you kissed me goodnight now, nobody would see."

He turned to face her, but he made no further move.

"Don't you want to?" she asked.

"Want to? I... Yes, Fran, I want to. I want to very much.

So much that...well, more than I can tell you. But—"

"Listen," she said—and she said it when she had taken his arms and put them around her and had brought her lips close to his. "Listen to me. Listen very carefully. When you want to kiss anybody else, you go into all those buts. When you want to kiss me, all you do is, you just...do...it."

Thankfully, gratefully, warmly and lingeringly, he did it.

Chapter Eleven

On the first night of the play, every line of which they now knew by heart, several members of the Chelsea and Campden Heights households were in evidence. Edmund, a fairly regular first-nighter, had no difficulty in getting seats for himself and for Fran. Ivor, applying to powerful friends of his grandmother, secured seats for Louisa and Frederica and himself in the dress circle. Mr. Bisley was in the upper circle. Welty, Euphonia and Teck were in the gallery.

They all looked very smart. Louisa's black-with-jet- beads, Frederica's midnight-blue-with-sequins proved that full dress for dowagers was what it had been fifty years ago. Welty wore a bright green embroidered waistcoat and a tight- fitting black suit, while Euphonia was in floral cotton in blinding shades of red, purple and green.

Mr. Sefton and Mrs. Bisley were not at the performance. She was visiting friends in the country, and Mr. Sefton had just recovered from a sharp attack of flu; tomorrow, Edmund was to drive him down to Somerset to stay with his widowed sister-in-law, Mrs. Hugh Sefton, for a period of recuperation. Ramon was unable to be present, since he was himself appearing with the Sevillanas at the Frank Eddleston Memorial Hall at Brixton. The company was playing to packed houses, but the Hall's seating accommodation was unfortunately limited to three hundred.

Manchester had shown no great enthusiasm for the play, and tonight's audience displayed no unusual tension or expectancy. Edmund saw familiar faces here and there, and in a box one that he had expected to see: Angela's. She looked down and saw him—and his companion; she raised a hand in greeting and he noticed on her wrist the bracelet he had given her on their engagement.

The curtain rose on a beautifully-designed Mediterranean harbour. Groups of fishermen stood about, doing little but talking a great deal; trouble seemed to be afoot, and through the excited babble of discussion, Jonathon, on stage when the curtain rose, watched from his lazy, hunched pose against an upturned boat. He looked very young, very immature—and very dangerous. He was inflammable material, and a good deal of heat was being generated round him. He seemed to exemplify a section of present-day youth, with nothing to do but wait for trouble. Nobody could deny that he was waiting with marked picturesqueness.

The first interval did not bring the scattered members of the households together; by pre-arrangement, they took up positions in the foyer and bars and asked one another, in clear and carrying tones, who the extraordinary young fisherman could be. A glance at the programme, and the name of Jonathon Dee

pronounced with equal clarity. Edmund heard Louisa's enthusiastic bellow up a crowded flight of stairs: so *HAND*some, so
unusu*AL*, so one might almost say com*PELL*ing.

Fran, he thought, carried the thing a little too far. It was
all right to move along the bar and make her point in a new
place, but she could have taken her drink with her, instead of
abandoning it and hurrying him away from his, and giving
him the trouble and expense of ordering others, only to be
hurried away again.

They were brought up, as he was aware they would be
before the interval was over, by Angela. He had watched her
without seeming to see her, and he knew well her way of pass-
ing through a crowd without any apparent haste or elbowing,
her patrician nose leading her unerringly to her quarry.

"Why...Edmund! Darling, how nice to see you! You know
Matt and Betsy, don't you?"

He did. But Fran didn't, and they didn't know Miss Nash.
Miss Francesca Nash: Miss Wilde, Lord and Lady Britling.
Lord Britling's monocle, Lady Britling's celebrated diamonds,
Angela's two-hundred-guinea gown against a white dress lent
by Leonie Rimbault. Wealth and glitter— against a white neck
and arms bare of ornament. Sophistication against...the word
welled up from Edmund's heart —against sweetness. It was
an outdated word and perhaps it was an outdated quality—but
she had it.

And she must, he thought, have had at least curiosity, but
it was subordinated to loyalty.

"How do you do? *Who,*" she asked them with breathless eagerness, "who for goodness sake was that man?"

"Man?" Her warmth seemed to have dislodged Lord Britling's monocle, and he adjusted it. "Which man?"

"There was only one," Fran said calmly. "He was young, and he didn't say anything at all. He just leaned against—"

"Oh, *that* young man! Well yes," Lady Britling was prepared to concede, "he was rather smouldering, in a way."

"Could you take your *eyes* off him?" Fran asked Angela, who plainly couldn't take her eyes off her. "I couldn't. I don't think they ought to have had him in the part, because he takes everybody's mind off everybody else in the play. Edmund, what did you say his name was?"

"He's Jonathon Dee. I hope," Edmund said, to his own surprise and pride, "he isn't having this effect on every woman in the audience. If he is, it's hard on their escorts."

"Ha-ha, Ha-ha, Ha-ha," laughed Lord Britling. "See what you mean. Yes, very hard; very hard indeed."

"I suppose," Angela asked Fran, and there was a patronising edge to her voice, "he's a friend of yours?"

"Of course!" Fran said instantly. "He's not only a friend, he's my star boarder, and soon he won't be a boarder any more because he'll be a star. Edmund"—she turned to him eagerly—"didn't you say Angela worked for a newspaper? You will," she begged Angela, swinging back to face her, "you *will* say lots of nice things about him, won't you? Put in that bit that Lady Britling said about him—about his smouldering. He didn't want people to think quite that, because he says he wants to be something quite new, and the smoulder type, he thinks, has had it long enough. What you *could* say is that he drew all eyes, which is true, or will be true before the end, because the woman comes in in the second act and she—"

"Fran—the bell," said Edmund. "If you want to see the second act, you'd better come and see it."

They walked back together, Fran between Lord and Lady Britling, Angela following with Edmund. Her eyebrows, upraised, were her only comment.

"I was away for Christmas," she said, "or I would have rung up and thanked you for your flowers."

He had sent them in contrition, because he was enjoying himself and because he was happy and because he had all but forgotten her—and also because he thought that some part of her might be hurt if he let Christmas pass without a word, without a sign.

"Did you enjoy New York?" he asked her.

"Yes." She gave him a sidelong glance. "We were to have gone together—remember?"

As man and wife. On the day Angela sailed, he had taken Fran out to dinner, and when he had left her at Campden Heights, he had dropped into Mr. Sefton's flat and had not remembered, until Mr. Sefton reminded him, that this was to have been his wedding night.

"You'd forgotten?" the old man asked.

"Yes."

After which, he remembered, he had made a long and rather incoherent speech about his happiness at being in what he called the Campden Heights circle. He also remembered Mr. Sefton's dry comment.

"It isn't so much a question of circles. It's a matter of sides. I'd like to know that you'd got that quite clear in your mind. There's the Angela side and there's the Fran side. You can be on one side or the other—but there's no bridge between them, so you've got to know pretty clearly which side you're on."

And now he was walking beside Angela into the darkened auditorium and wondering whether she had slipped her hand into his because of the difficulty of finding the way, or for old times' sake, or because she had assessed the competition—and dismissed it.

He saw, as he led Fran back to their seats, his Uncle Robert trying to attract his attention. He looked the other way, and in the next interval, kept Fran in her seat.

When the final curtain dropped, there were no demonstrations, for or against. Edmund steered Fran towards the exit with a skill and swiftness that defeated the efforts of both Uncle Robert and Angela to reach them. He waited for Louisa and Frederica and put them into a taxi. Ivor went off to a free supper at the Rimbault. Mr. Bisley had promised to drop in and give Mr. Sefton an account of the play's reception. Of

Teck, Welty and Euphonia there was no sign.

Edmund and Fran had supper at his house; Welty had laid out a cold meal and a jugful of a drink he called rum-and-some-other-things. They ate and drank by the drawing room fire, talking of Jonathon and the play—and then Fran curled her feet under her on the sofa and looked up at Edmund.

"Tell me how you felt," she said.

"About Jonathon?"

"No, of course not about Jonathon. About Angela. How could you ever even *like* her, let alone fall in love? What did you let her hold your hand for? I saw her clinging to you. Did you feel anything?"

"Have you ever heard of a certain code?"

"Chivalry? Didn't that go out with armour? You mean you won't tell me?"

"I mean that it's getting late, and if you don't let me take you home, you won't be up early for that nice solitary half-hour you like so much."

"If it's a choice between a nice half hour here, or a nice half hour in the kitchen tomorrow morning, I choose this one. Are you too tired? Oh—you've got to get up early, haven't you, to drive Mr. Sefton down to...where's the place?"

"Roseleigh. Somerset."

"It sounds pretty. Do you know it?"

"I've been there twice, when my father was alive. It's only a sort of hamlet—population about two hundred. Mr. Sefton's sister-in-law is a widow and she lives alone in a very small house on a very steep hill."

"Will she look after him nicely?"

"Yes. She'd look after him permanently if he cared to go and live down there, but he won't; it's too isolated; too quiet. He only goes there when he's feeling really low."

"When'll you be back?"

"Tomorrow evening. All I'm doing is driving him down and coming straight back. He's not fit enough to go by train —and the train would only take him part of the way."

"Do you feel too tired to talk?"

"No, but—"

"Then let's talk. Do you know how much better you are at talking than when I first met you? That's odd, isn't it? You'd think, wouldn't you, that after meeting a family that talks as much as ours does, you'd never be able to open your mouth again? But you do, and you keep it open for whole paragraphs. Edmund...I'm feeling awfully happy..."

"How much of that rum stuff did you drink?"

"Hardly any. It isn't the rum stuff; it's something much more heady. It's what Ivor calls twinklers—all those twinklers I've been seeing tonight twinkling in women's heads and on their necks and arms. You've taken an awful risk—you've introduced a simple country girl to the dangers and the delights of London, and it's gone to her head. From now on, I want one first night a week, with a bit of the peerage thrown in, and a spiteful beauty with claws just to keep my feet on the carpet." She stretched her arms above her head in a gesture of utter contentment. "Oh Edmund the Forth, I'm so glad, so glad, so glad I met you!"

He wanted to say that he was glad he had met her, too, but the line sounded too much like some of the dialogue that Jonathon had been almost glad not to have to speak. He went to the sofa and drew her to her feet.

"You're going home," he said.

"Why?" she protested, sitting down again. "I've got things to say. Things to ask you."

"What things?"

"Sit down and I'll tell you."

He sat on a chair opposite, and looked across at her. "Well?"

Her mood seemed to have changed; she spoke seriously. "About tonight," she said, and hesitated. "I suppose..."

"You suppose?"

"Well, I wouldn't live anywhere else or be anything else, but doesn't it worry you a bit when I mention a boarding house? In front of people like Angela, I mean."

"No, it doesn't worry me in the least."

"It would have done at one time, wouldn't it?"

"Only because I was rather out of date."

"I thought you wouldn't tell Mr. Sefton about the tele-gram—but you did. Why?"

"Because he kept giving me credit for having offered Louisa and Frederica a home, and I didn't want to claim it."

"You knew lots of people in the theatre tonight, but you didn't go and talk to them. Why?"

"I preferred to stay with you."

She got to her feet, and he rose and stood waiting. She came close to him and put her hands on his arms and looked up at him and spoke slowly.

"Are you sure you're not lonely, just with us—Ivor and Jonathon and Ramon and me and the rest?"

"I'm quite sure."

"You don't feel, any more, that you're a hundred and eight years old?"

"Sometimes," he said. "I do, for example, at this moment."

"Why?"

"Because you look very, very young and..."

He said no more. She had slipped her arms about his neck and was drawing his head down to hers until their lips met and clung. His arms went round her and the room, the house, the world dissolved slowly, and left him suspended in timeless space.

When he released her at last, he took her hands and laid them against his cheeks.

"Fran," he said huskily, "I love you very, very much."

He heard her long, deep sigh.

"I love you too," she said. She laid her head against his

chest and put her arms protectively about him. "Oh Edmund, Edmund, Edmund," she said with loving resignation, "why didn't you make yourself harder to catch?"

He drove her back to her house. A man could drive, he had heard, when drunk—and he was drunk with happiness. She was beside him. She was his—Francesca Rosamund Annabelle Nash.

So much for plans, he reflected. Mice and men... He had planned to marry Angela. He had planned a wedding date that would be a good time to leave the office, and a good time to give Mr. and Mrs. Yates a holiday. He had planned this, and that, and the other.

Tonight, there was no plan. There was only the present—and Fran.

The Campden Heights house was in darkness; he opened the door with her key, held her for a moment in his arms and then went reluctantly away. He drove home and saw lights in Louisa and Frederica's flat and thought that he would go down and tell them—and then decided that he would not. He wanted to be alone.

He put his car into the garage and walked out into the road and towards his front door. To his surprise, he heard Louisa bidding a guest goodnight, but heard no answering voice. Her door closed and there were footsteps—and then Edmund saw Teck coming up to pavement level, and understood why he had not responded to the farewells.

Ginger wine.

He would, he realised, have to take the old man home. He went up to him and took his arm and led him gently along the road to the garage. It was an unseasonal night—wet, but almost warm. As he reached the garage, he saw the light of the house next door go on; the front door opened, and Lord Wilversham appeared, seeing Uncle Robert off.

"Well, hello there, Edmund." Uncle Robert was in his most expansive mood; Edmund surmised that Lord Wilversham must be proving very useful indeed. "This is my nephew Edmund, Willy; neighbour of yours, as I told you. Just home, Edmund?"

"Just going out," Edmund said. "I'm taking somebody home."

"Ha—casualty, I see," said Lord Wilversham, coming down a few steps for a better look. "Friend of yours?"

"In a way," said Edmund.

" *'Fallen from his high estate,'* " mourned Teck.

" *'And weltering in his blood:*
Deserted at his utmost need By those...' "

'My word! Not a happy drunk," Lord Wilversham commented. "But poetic. That's Dryden, isn't it?'

"At midnight," said Uncle Robert, "I don't know Dryden from Donne. And that's midnight striking now. Goodnight, Willy, and thanks for the drink. Hope you enjoyed the show."

"Very much, thanks. Pity you phoned for a taxi; your

nephew could have given you a lift."

The taxi drove up; Uncle Robert drove away. Edmund backed his car out of the garage, settled Teck into it, and Lord Wilversham stood on his doorstep to wave them off.

At Campden Heights, Edmund got Teck out of the car and groped in his pockets for a latchkey.

"Bottom pocket of his waistcoat," came in Mr. Bisley's high, thin tones. "That's where he keeps it."

He was standing at the gap in the laurels that led to his own doorway. He came forward, found the key, opened the door and held it while Edmund entered with Teck. Teck, now too sleepy to recite, submitted quietly to having his shoes taken off and the counterpane drawn gently over him.

Outside once more, Edmund stopped at the gate and turned to look up at Fran's window. He had no idea how long he stood there, but the sound of Mr. Bisley's voice made him start violently.

"Oh—I thought you'd gone in," he said.

"No. Waiting to hear what you thought of the play," said the old man.

"I didn't think it was up to much. Did you?"

"No. Just been telling Sefton so. You're driving him down to Somerset tomorrow, I hear. Today, rather."

"Yes."

"Do him good. Going to marry her?" he enquired without the slightest pause.

211

"Yes, I am," Edmund said.

"Thought you would. You've got your mother's eye for a good thing. 'Night. Sleep well."

Edmund slept not at all, and the next morning tucked Mr. Sefton warmly into the car and set off for Somerset. The drive was a silent one; Edmund was too happy, Mr. Sefton too miserable to be in conversational mood; the setting was not one in which to divulge the news of an engagement.

Once in Somerset, any exchange other than shouts would have been impossible, for almost without warning, they ran into a storm of shattering violence. One moment they were driving through a drizzle that showed no sign of becoming heavier—and the next, there was a blinding flash of lightning followed almost immediately by a thunderclap. The sound seemed to tear open the heavens, for Edmund found himself driving against hailstones that drove savagely against the windscreen and the windows and shut out the view with the effectiveness of a blizzard.

It could not, he thought, last—but as he crawled mile after mile, the downpour showed no sign of abating. Roads turned from damp tarmac to slippery sheets of glass and then to rivers. The car plunged through water that got deeper and deeper, and there was nothing to do but go on and be thankful for the warmth and comfort within the car.

Progress was painfully slow, and Edmund's spirits fell. He wanted to be back in London by nightfall; at this rate, if he got back at all, it would be too late to see Fran...

He went on and on, unable to make out signposts through the downpour, but guided by Mr. Sefton's knowledge of the route. The wind howled more and more loudly; when darkness fell, conditions were such that he realised it would be impossible to do more than grope a way to their destination; with the countryside a lake, he would have to ask Mrs. Hugh to let him bed down on the sofa for the night.

He was glad that the cottage was on a hill; the steep, narrow road was difficult to negotiate, but at least it was not under water. There were lights—a few lights—below them, and a bright, welcoming one when they reached the house at the top.

Sheltering under a huge golf umbrella and several coats, he and the cheerful, loud-voiced Mrs. Hugh got Mr. Sefton up the path and into the warm, comfortable little sitting-room.

"My goodness gracious!" she exclaimed. "I didn't expect to see you! Did you ever know anything like it?"

"When did it start here?" Mr. Sefton enquired from his nest of rugs.

"About midday. It got darker and darker, and then—this. I was worrying about you both, because there hasn't been a tradesman's van up this way, and I think all the roads down below are flooded. I can't find out for certain, because the phone's gone off. George, don't get too comfortable; you're going straight up to a nice, warm bed. Edmund, you won't be able to go anywhere tonight."

Or, he found, the next night—or the next. He woke early on the first morning, drew back the sitting-room curtains and

213

looked out over an endless sheet of water. The traffic below was moving, but it was water traffic; in what had been the main street of Roseleigh, home-made rafts, barrels, zinc tubs and wooden washing tubs were being paddled from house to house. The storm had ended, but the rain continued; it was quiet now, but steady and persistent.

"Well now!" said Mrs. Hugh. "It's lucky for you men that I keep a good stock of tinned stuff in the house. It's going to be as good as a siege."

If he had not been longing to get home, Edmund would have been able to enjoy it. He made his way down the hill in the late Hugh's waders, and helped to fish out provisions from the three small shops and load them on to rafts and distribute them to the line of straggling, half-inundated houses. He carried children shoulder-high and organised a convoy of rafts and tubs to float out to a large half-ruined building which had the advantage of having two floors well above water. Rugs and blankets were found, paraffin stoves lit and volunteer cooks set to prepare hot meals on a long- disused, rusty oil cooker. Two frail old ladies were ferried to the foot of the hill and taken up in Edmund's car to be looked after by Mrs. Hugh.

By midday, the people of Roseleigh were as comfortable as could be expected. They were cut off, as no doubt many other neighbouring places were cut off, but they had food, the cows had been milked and barrels of water and beer had been floated out to the camping families. There was nothing more to be done; the rain would stop, the waters would subside and they would be able to read about themselves in the newspapers.

Edmund had arrived on Friday. It was Tuesday morning before the roads were once more fit for wheeled traffic. He said goodbye to Mr. Sefton and Mrs. Hugh, received the blessings of the grateful occupants of the houses below, and sped back to London.

He was in a hurry, and he went without pause through the hall of the office building, avoided the lift with its cargo of passengers eager to question him about the floods, ran up several flights of stairs and walked straight through the office to his own room. Swift as was his passage through the outer office, however, he had time to note an unusual air of tension.

"What's the matter with them all out there?" he asked Miss Brady with a smile, as he entered his room. "Did they think I was drowned in the storm?"

Miss Brady was standing on the other side of his desk, looking at him with no change in her calm, stolid expression. Her unusual hesitation in answering, however, made him wonder whether they had lost a valuable client.

"I couldn't telephone," he said. "The lines were all down —but you knew where I was, and you must have known I was marooned."

"Yes, we knew, Mr. Forth," she said. "The papers have been full of it. But ..."

"Has something happened?" he asked.

"Didn't you see Mr. Robert Forth as you came in?"

"No, I didn't. Is he here?"

"Yes. He wouldn't go away. He said you were sure to be here soon, as the roads were clear."

"Then you can tell him I'm back. You can also tell him I'm in a hurry."

"Perhaps it would be better," Miss Brady said, "if you listened to what I have to say before you see him. I think you should, Mr. Forth."

"Well, go on."

"It's about your cousins—Miss Louisa and Miss Frederica. They came in to the office to see me."

"When?"

"On Saturday morning."

"What on earth did they want?" Edmund asked in surprise.

"Money," said Miss Brady.

A feeling of uneasiness crept over him.

"*Money?*" he echoed.

"Yes. They said that you were the only person they could apply to, and as you were away, they thought that I could let them have it—in your name, of course. They wanted it at once. Urgently."

He stared at her, the uneasiness becoming a chilly feeling. Money...urgently...

"How much did they want?" he asked.

"One hundred pounds."

For some moments he was unable to speak.

"Do you know...did they say what they wanted the money for?" he asked at last.

"Yes. For bail," said Miss Brady.

Chapter Twelve

It had never occurred to Edmund that his secretary's self-possession could be anything but admirable—but when bad news had to be communicated, he now realised, it was better to receive some kind of preparation, and a little more expression on Miss Brady's face would have given it to him. As it was, he was left with the feeling that she had knocked all the breath out of his body.

He sat down slowly and squared his shoulders.

"All right. Let's have it," he said. "They came in and asked for one hundred pounds—for bail. And you gave it to them."

"Yes, Mr. Forth. I was sure that you would want me to. But Mr. Robert Forth was very angry with me when he—"

"How did he hear about it?"

"I don't know, Mr Forth. He was in the office almost the whole of yesterday, waiting for you in case you might have been able to get back. He got on to the police in Somerset to ask about the state of the roads. I put him into the waiting-room, but he didn't seem to want to stay there, and that's why I thought you might have met him as you came in just now. I'm glad you didn't, because I wanted to talk to you first."

"Well, talk," directed Edmund. "One hundred pounds—for bail."

"Yes. You see, Mr. Forth, it was—"

She stopped. The door had been flung open without ceremony, and Uncle Robert appeared on the threshold. His face was dark with anger.

"Well, here you are at last," he informed Edmund. "A fine time to choose to put yourself out of reach."

Edmund nodded to Miss Brady, and she went out and closed the door behind her.

"Sit down, won't you?" he said.

His uncle sat down and stared belligerently across the desk.

"I've been expecting something like this," he said. "It was too much to hope that they'd keep out of the news for long. I wish to Heaven I'd clapped them into an institution years ago and left them there."

"If you mean a mental institution," Edmund said coldly, "you would have had to have grounds."

"Well, I've got grounds now. They're in a pretty mess, and if you don't look out, you'll be in it too. That's what I've been waiting all this time to tell you. I've been shuttling between your house and your blasted office half yesterday and the whole of today, and you can thank your stars I'm in touch with the kind of people who can tip me off when necessary.

219

Mind you, this is all absolutely between you and me. If it leaked out, old Dilling would be in serious trouble."

"Dilling. Sir Clive Dilling?"

"Who else? After all, this is a family matter, and he married a Forth. He got hold of me on the phone and asked me to go up and see him, and he gave it to me in the strictest confidence. I must say it was very good of him, because—"

"What," Edmund asked, "did he give you?"

"Simply another version of the story that Angela told me later on—but of course, in his position, he—"

"Wouldn't it be better," suggested Edmund, "to begin at the beginning?"

His uncle stared at him in astonishment.

"Didn't that secretary of yours tell you that Louisa and Frederica had—"

"She told me that she had given them a hundred pounds which they'd asked for—for bail. At that point, you came in."

"So you know nothing?"

"Nothing." Edmund tried to subdue his mounting panic. "I'd be glad to know what's happened."

"You won't be glad at all. It appears that they went bail for some old ex-jailbird they'd got to know—don't ask me how. They—"

"Ex-jailbird?"

"Yes. Let me tell it without interruptions, will you? There's much worse to come. This fellow lives in a place somewhere in the Campden district, and he made off with a bracelet belonging to a minor actress of sorts—can't remember her name, but she was in that play that opened the other night. Angela tells me that the girl you were with might have some sort of tie-up with this, but that's beside the point. Roberta Clunes—that's the woman's name—put the matter in the hands of the police, and when Louisa and Frederica heard of it, they went to the police and made a statement to the effect that they could prove that the man was nowhere near the house at the time the bracelet was stolen. They—"

"But—"

"Look, don't keep breaking in, will you? The thing's confused enough as it is. They went to the police and made a statement, and that's where Dilling comes in. Scotland Yard doesn't hear at once about every tom-and-jerry little case that breaks in some outlying district of London—but there were certain facts about this case which made it outstanding, or peculiar, or noteworthy, whichever way you want to look at it. Because four other people came forward and made four entirely separate statements and gave the man four entirely different alibis. With Louisa and Frederica's, that makes five. Five statements, all sworn—and ail different. They're all sticking to their stories and they're all prepared to get up in court and swear to them and stick to them there. All five. Well, old Dilling got wind of this, and when he heard the name Forth, he pricked up his ears. I don't mind telling you now that family connections apart, I hope, with Lord Wilversham's backing, to stand for Parliament for old Dilling's constituency, so naturally he doesn't want me even remotely mixed up in anything of this kind. He found out that the two old ladies were Louisa and Frederica, and with that, he asked me up to his place for a drink, and in absolute secrecy, told me that I'd better get the old ladies to retire with dignity. Old ladies, he said, often get these waves of compassion, and it's no doubt a great credit to them, but the police get a bit tired of them. When I left Dilling, I went straight along to see Louisa and Frederica; I'm damn sure they were in, but they wouldn't answer the door. You've got to get hold of them at once, Edmund, and you've got to make them withdraw that statement. Think of it! They actually said they'd had this fellow at their flat—at *your* flat—this ex-thief, late on the night of Thursday, throughout the time he was said to have stolen the ring or the bracelet or whatever it was. I've had a lot of shocks in my time, but I didn't think I'd live to hear a couple of my relations proposing to get up in a sordid case and make spectacles of themselves."

Bail...not for themselves, but for an ex-thief.

An alibi...for Thursday night.

He saw his uncle rise, and heard him speaking irritably.

"Well, don't just sit there, Edmund. Get a move on. Get out to Chelsea and make those two retract that statement—and fast."

"I'm afraid I can't do that," Edmund said.

There was a short silence.

"I don't know what the hell you mean by that," Uncle Robert said flatly at last. "Are you trying to say you won't do it?"

"I can't do it. Their statement is true."

"True?" The word was a jeer. "And what about all the other four statements ? True too, I suppose?"

"If they're different, they can't be true. But this man was certainly at the flat on Thursday night. I saw him there. And so," he added, "did you."

"Me!" came from the other man out of a long, stunned silence. *"Me?"*

"The man you saw me with on Thursday night was this man called Teck who once served a prison sentence. He had been to see Louisa and Frederica, and he must have been there for a short time at any rate, because they had given him some of their ginger wine. As he's not a drinker, and as it's lethal stuff, it had the effect on him that you noticed."

Uncle Robert gave a brief, savage laugh.

"And you think you're going to get me into court to say that? You think you're going to mix me—*me!*—up in this? Do you think for one moment that I'll corroborate their statement—or your statement?"

"If you won't," said Edmund, "I think Lord Wilversham will."

At the look on his uncle's face, he got slowly to his feet. People, he remembered, got apoplexy. He wasn't sure how it came on, but he felt certain that it was preceded by the kind of look Uncle Robert was wearing now. It was an about-to- burst look.

There was nothing to do, he decided, but wait. If he burst, he burst. There was nothing to do but regret deeply the fact that this overfed, blustering, self-seeking old man was a relation, and a close one. There was nothing to do but wait for him to recover. He waited, and thought of Fran. He wanted to see her—so much that he had difficulty in preventing himself from putting Uncle Robert aside and walking out of the room.

It was his uncle who walked out. Without another word, he turned on his heel and strode to the door and left it swinging behind him.

Edmund waited until he could be certain that he had left the building; then he went out and brought the lift up again and had stepped into it and closed the door when he saw through the grille the face of Miss Brady.

"Mr. Forth, Miss Wilde is here—she wants to see you."

"You just missed me," said Edmund, and put his finger on the ground floor button.

Then he withdrew it, opened the door and stepped out beside Miss Brady.

"All right," he said. "I'll see her. Bring her along to my room."

It was easy, he told himself, going back, to know what Angela had come for. If the facts of the case had spread as far as Sir Clive Dilling, it was a hundred to one that some eager news-hound had got on to something—and had put it on Angela's desk. She would be able to get a fuller, a far clearer picture than Uncle Robert; she had seen a girl at the theatre, a girl who had spoken of boarders...

He was standing behind his desk when Miss Brady opened the door and closed it again behind Angela. For a moment there was a pause, and then she spoke.

"I'm so glad I was in time to see you, Edmund," she said. "I was afraid I'd just missed you."

He knew that tone well, he reminded himself. She had used it when she wasn't sure how he was going to react; it was a non-committal tone that could be turned to sweet or not so sweet, according. But she was beautiful, he admitted, and hadn't she, after all, once had everything he wanted, everything he had asked of her? It wasn't her fault that he had suddenly, inexplicably, begun to ask for things that she hadn't got—a heart, for instance.

"Sit down, Angela," he said.

"No. I haven't time, and there isn't much to say. I met your uncle downstairs and he—"

"I'm glad he got downstairs," Edmund heard himself saying coldly. "I was afraid he might have a stroke on the way down. Have you come to ask me to make Louisa and Frederica withdraw their statements? That was why he was here. He didn't want them to get mixed up in anything."

"Even he, Edmund, didn't know quite how much there is to get mixed up in. I do—and that's why I came to see you."

"I give evidence and clear an old man who's been wrongfully accused of stealing. What more is there in it than that? Uncle Robert made a great stir about the other four statements, but as soon as they're withdrawn, the—"

"But that's just the point. They're not going to be withdrawn. Our reporters have been down to Campden Heights and have talked to the people who made the statements, and each and every one of them maintained that their statement is true, and will stand. Nobody's going to withdraw anything."

"Simply because there was no corroboration of the statement made by Louisa and Frederica. I can supply it."

"There *was* corroboration. I don't have to tell you, Edmund, that I'm being extremely unprofessional, not to say unethical in telling you this. I'm doing it because you're not in a position, and I *am,* to know exactly what will happen if this case goes to court with those other four statements still—"

"What corroboration?" he asked.

"A man called Bisley came forward to say that he saw you bringing the man Teck home shortly after midnight—drunk. So that you only had to fill in the gap: that you drove the man home from your cousins' flat. The reporters were quite sure you did, long before you told your uncle so. So what you have to understand is that although your cousins' statement is true, and is well substantiated, the other four are not going to be withdrawn. So what you're involving yourself in isn't a minor

226

case in which you merely do your duty as a good citizen and give evidence that will clear a suspect. You're getting involved in a huge, nation-wide joke. This case, with five sworn statements, is going to be news—big news. We all like a laugh at times, but this time, you're going to help us to get one. Once the Press is free to comment, the thing will make headlines. It'll be splashed across the front pages— certainly across our front page. You don't know how deep reporters can dig once they've got the scent—but *I* know. They're digging now—and they're bringing up some prizes. I suppose you know that one of the statements has been made by a young man calling himself Ivor Breck?"

"His name **is** Ivor Breck."

"Grandson of the Countess of Dellston. Can you imagine her feelings when, in due course, there's a rush to interview her? And the man Bisley is living under an assumed name— did you know that?"

"No."

"His real name is Wilfred van Willans, and his pictures fetch astronomical figures at the sales."

Edmund said nothing. His mind had swung back to his first meeting with old Mr. Bisley. Sesimbra? No. Nazare? No. Bare. Stark. In other words, the picture that hung on his own wall at Chelsea. Mr. Bisley of the withered hands— Wilfred van Willans. Mr. Bisley, living with his wife at Number 11 Campden Heights while his pictures made fortunes for their vendors...

227

With an effort, he brought his mind back to Angela.

"The reason those statements haven't been withdrawn," he said, "is because the people who made them are waiting to talk to me and to make absolutely certain that the alibi will stand up. Once I make them see that it will, they'll all take back whatever it was they swore to."

"And now we come to the point," said Angela. "Why *all?*"

"I don't understand what you mean," he said.

"It's quite simple." She put her hands on the desk and leaned on them and spoke slowly and patiently—as to an idiot, he thought. "I'm here to help you, but you've got to help yourself too. You're on the edge of a rather dirty duck- pond, and I'm trying to help you to skirt it instead of falling into it. So listen to me: You know that this man is innocent; you can prove it—if necessary. But *is* it necessary? That is, is it necessary for *you* to prove it? Only one statement is required. One cast-iron alibi will do the trick. In my opinion, the actor Jonathon Dee ought to be the one to choose—he's the one most likely to keep his head under cross-examination. The other statements—*all* the other statements can be withdrawn."

"The statement made by my cousins is true."

"And being true, gives you the assurance that this man didn't steal the bracelet. Knowing that, all you have to do is make sure that Jonathon Dee can safely undergo cross- examination, can stick to the alibi he claimed for the man, can get him acquitted. That, after all, is the object of the exercise, isn't it: simply and solely to make certain that the man is cleared, exonerated, acquitted. You've just said that you can make those other four people withdraw their statements. If you've enough influence to make them do that, you can persuade Jonathon Dee to be the one to go into court. And then you and your cousins can keep clear of the whole thing. Do you see?"

There was silence. He found nothing to say, but perhaps his face—as Fran had once told him—was more expressive than he realised. When Angela spoke again, her tone had changed to one halfway between amusement and contempt.

"You've a rather special interest in this case, of course," she said. "I didn't go into it too deeply with your uncle, as I wasn't sure how seriously you were involved." She leaned against the desk and swung her beautiful black gloves. "How did you first get into the boarding house?" she asked. "And how deeply involved are you with the Nash girl? Can I give you a little advice, Edmund?"

"I think," he said, "it comes too late."

"Well, it's good advice. I know you, I suppose, as well as anybody, and one of the things I know about you is that you don't fit into that set-up. She's a pretty little thing and she's got a certain kind of talkative charm and there's no harm in your losing your head—a little. But I really think it's time you extri-cated yourself. She was amusing, and it was fun, and men are only men—but you can go too far down any road, and you're already too far down this one. How do you think I felt when I saw your name mixed up in this...this farce? You can't say I haven't been patient, but you've really carried this far enough.

What's more, you're playing out of character. You're a sane, intelligent man who knows perfectly well where his real interests lie, and mixing yourself up in this mess merely makes you look a fool. It isn't your age group, you know. And if you won't think of yourself, why don't you think of me?"

There was a pause.

"How," he asked, "do you come into this?"

"How? I'm *in* it! Doesn't every single soul in my office, from the highest to the lowest, know perfectly well that I was engaged to you, that we quarrelled and that I've shown remarkable patience in waiting while you worked this midwinter madness out of your system? Do you think I won't be dragged into this mess too? And do you imagine that if you involved me in publicity of that kind, I would ever speak to you again, or allow you to speak to me? A quarrel is a quarrel—but this would really be the finish. Surely you see that?"

In the long silence that followed, he saw a great many things. And the clearest of them all was that he had not been expected to take the return of his ring as final. She had been prepared for a reconciliation—on her own terms. She was standing here now uttering what sounded like a threat—but he was quite sure that whether she was involved in publicity or not, there would be a loophole through which he could make his way back to her. For he was, as Mr. Sefton had told him, what she wanted, just as once she had been what he wanted: a figure modelled to a certain pattern, or a figurehead suitably impressive to ride the prow of the matrimonial ship.

She had never, he knew, roused strong feelings in him. They were strong now—but they were feelings of pity.

"You're not," he heard her say, "in a very reasonable frame of mind. I can see I'm wasting my time. Perhaps you'll see me out?"

They walked through the office, past rows of studiously-bent heads, and waited in silence for the lift. It came, and he opened the door for her and she got in.

"Don't come down with me," she said. "I know the way out—and I know when to take it." She smiled, and the smile was her mother's. "You won't expect me, will you, to tone down the publicity?"

"No, I won't," he said.

"Then I'm glad we understand one another—at last."

The lift bore her downward—and with her, he knew, went the last of his old world. As he drove, some minutes later and with complete disregard of safety rules, to Campden Heights, he knew with complete certainty which side he was on.

And if he did not know, the next half-hour was to show him.

The door opened before he had time to ring the bell—but it was not Fran who answered it.

"Come in," Ivor said, and drew him inside. "We've been waiting for you."

"Where's Fran?"

Ivor ushered him into the drawing-room and closed the

231

door.

"Fran," he said, "is out. Here are Leonie and myself, Jonathon and Ramon, assembled, waiting for you. We sent Fran to your house. I had my Baker Street runners out tracking your movements, and as soon as we knew you were heading in this direction, we told Fran you were heading towards Chelsea, and we sent her there to meet you like a dutiful future wife. If congratulations are in order, we all offer them —but what we want to do most of all at this moment is to talk to you."

"To find out," Jonathon said, "how much you'd heard."

"We wanted," Leonie said, "to speak to you alone. That is, we did not wish Fran to be here."

Edmund looked from one to the other.

"Four separate statements," he said. "If you were going to lie, why didn't you get together and make it a concerted effort?"

"You're talking in the light of several days later," Ivor said. "You're being wise after the event. You're late for the real fireworks."

"You went to your office," Jonathon said. "I suppose your secretary told you that Louisa and Frederica had gone there to get money?"

"Yes. She—"

"We couldn't raise it," Ivor said. "Me with my titled grandmother, Leonie with her well-heeled Papa; we couldn't scrape together one hundred pounds. Not fast, that is. But Louisa didn't hesitate. 'We'll go to the office,' she said. 'I shall tell them who we are and they will give us the money in Edmund's name.' Which they did. Thanks. And now: what else did your secretary tell you?"

"Never mind what she told me," Edmund said. "Begin at the beginning."

"The beginning," Jonathon said, "was in this house. It was after the first night of the play, and there was the usual first-night party. I wasn't with the stars, of course; I was with a bunch of the second, third and fourth grades of the cast. We went to a dive in Kensington and had a few drinks and made a lot of noise, to convince ourselves that the show hadn't been as lousy as it had seemed from our side of the footlights. Well, I left at about eleven-thirty and was on my way to the bus, when this Roberta Clunes caught me up. In case you don't remember, she was the girl who was jilted in Act One and drowned herself in Act Two. She'd been making a ruddy nuisance of herself all through rehearsals and all the way through the tryout. There are women you can shake off and women you can't, and she was the original limpet. I can't give you the usual line about wondering what she sees in me, because I know; she told me, several times. So she caught me up on my way to the bus, and tried to head me off to her flat. I had a bottle of champagne with me, which I was bringing back to the house to open when we'd all got back; it struck me that the quickest way of getting rid of her was to come back here, give her a drink and hope that somebody'd come in and lead her to the door and see her

233

off the premises. But when we got here, nobody was in. The empty house seemed to send Roberta's temperature up several degrees, and she got a bit out of hand. It isn't wise for an actor on his way up to get on the wrong side of a girl who's got the producer's ear, but I made her see that this wasn't going to be what she'd hoped. She got a bit abusive— and it was just about then that she pulled off this bracelet and showed it to me."

He paused, and continued the story leaning against the mantelpiece, staring moodily into the fire.

"We were in the hall—on our way out. I think she thought that when I saw the bracelet—which she said was worth a packet, and had been given to her by some Italian prince she didn't care to name—I would have got jealous, and taken a new view of her charms. It's an old gag, off the same shelf as pretending to be pregnant so's you'll marry them. I said Pretty-Pretty, and went into the kitchen to get my coat, where I'd left it when I got the glasses for the drink. She followed me in, and what followed was painful but, from her point of view, unproductive. She got rather shrill, and I told her to keep it down or she'd wake Teck, and she said 'Oh, he's the one who did time?' That shook me; I didn't see how she could have known, but she lives not far from here, and the tradespeople, she said, know all about him.

"Well, I convinced her that she'd wasted her evening, and I rang for a taxi, but I couldn't get one, and so I walked with her to the corner and stood waiting for one. And just as we got there, she gave a shriek and yelled: 'My bracelet! I left it in the hall!' So back we came—"

"What time was this?" Edmund asked.

"Just about twelve. I opened the door, we came in. No bracelet. Is she sure she left it there? She's quite sure. She put it down—she said—on the hall table when she followed me out into the kitchen, and when we left the house, she was too upset to remember it. I looked here and there, but I couldn't locate it, and then she took my breath away by saying that she knew quite well where it went: it had been stolen. By whom? By Teck. I took her to Teck's room and showed her that there was nobody in it, but she said that didn't prove anything. I was a bit suspicious, by this time, about whether she'd lost the thing at all, but I could hardly search her, so I made her come out with me again and we covered the ground, searching. No bracelet. We came back to the house again and—"

"What time?" Edmund asked.

"I don't know. I'd lost count of time. But Teck was in his room—sleeping it off. And I wasn't surprised when Roberta rang me up to tell me she'd laid a charge."

"And then?" Edmund asked.

Ivor took up the tale.

"Fran," he said, "nearly went out of her mind. She was certain, as we were all certain, that Teck didn't come into it— but she was frightened of having his record dragged up and held against him. We had Teck in and told him the whole story, but we knew—because we knew how drink always blotted everything out—that he wouldn't be able to tell us anything except the fact that he knew nothing about it. We all decided that he'd met somebody after the show and got let in for a drink—but it was all guess work."

"And the thing is," Jonathon said, "nobody'll ever see that bracelet again. It's done what Roberta wanted it to do: got her own back on me, and brought her a bit of cheap publicity. Edmund, I'm no judge of jewellery, but if that thing was worth ten-and-sixpence, I'll give up my hopes of ever getting to the top. It was a cheap, come-by-the-dozen affair. She told me it was given to her by this prince; in her statement to the police, it turned into an old family jewel, handed down—and down. I asked her to come to this house —she says. Why didn't she look for the bracelet on the hall table as she left the house? She was too upset. She didn't say why, but the inference is clear: I all but raped her. I'm only surprised she didn't tell them that I swiped the bracelet, but the fact of having a ready-made suspect in the house was too good to miss."

"So she made her charge—and then?" Edmund asked.

"Well, we were all present at what's usually breakfast," Ivor said, "but nobody was eating. Fran was crying, and we'd never seen her cry before, and it had a most peculiar effect on all of us. I myself would have given anything in the world to make her happy again, but all I could think of was making sure that nobody could pin the thing on to Teck, so on my way to the shop I dropped into a police station and told them I wanted to make a statement—and did. It was a very good statement, and I'm proud of it. I only wish I'd tried my hand at being a writer. The words just flowed. Pure fiction, and all effortless."

"And when he came home and told me what he'd done," Jonathon said, "I told him what I'd done. And Ramon and Leonie told us what they'd done. I made my statement to the police round the corner, and I'd like to see Roberta Clunes' face when she hears what's in it, because every word of it contradicts what she said."

"And my cousins?" Edmund asked.

"Came in in the middle of everything," Jonathon told him, "and listened with great astonishment and at the end looked at one another and Louisa said: 'But my *dears*, Teck was with us!' Well, naturally we all thought they were rallying round, as we'd tried to do, to save Teck. They went on to say that their statement would have greater weight with the police— which we all strongly but privately doubted. Having made statements which we all felt were pretty good, we weren't too keen on having a couple of seemingly crackpot— excuse me, Edmund—old girls tottering in and saying they'd done the deed and could lead the police to the corpse. And Fran, naturally, was sick with terror because they were about to drag the name of Forth through the mud. But nothing any of us could say could stop the old girls. They went to the police. And just about the time they were making their statement, old Bisley came in, heard the whole story—and staggered us all by saying that he'd seen you bringing Teck back to the house full of the old ladies' ginger wine. That finished Fran off completely;

237

first Louisa and Frederica involved, and then you. That was the end."

"Not quite the end," Edmund said. "You've all got to go round to your various police stations and take back all you said. In other words, you've got to retract your statements."

There was a long silence. They were all, he saw, too surprised for speech; four pairs of eyes gazed at him in the utmost astonishment.

"Retract?" said Ivor at last. "Why retract?"

"Why? Because don't you see," said Edmund, "that Teck now has a completely satisfactory alibi?"

"What's satisfactory about it?" demanded Jonathon.

"Who," asked Ivor, "is going to take Louisa and Frederica seriously?"

"I am corroborating their statement," Edmund reminded them.

"Quite so," said Ivor. "What else, people will ask, could you do but back up your crackpot—excuse me again— cousins?"

"We know you're telling the truth, and they're telling the truth," said Jonathon, "but who—apart from our own small circle—is going to believe it's the truth?"

"Nobody," said Leonie. "Nobody at all."

"Nobody," said Ramon.

"You either have to label your dear old cousins mentally unstable, or uphold what they say," said Jonathon. "So you back them."

"So can my Uncle Robert," said Edmund. "He saw me with Teck."

Again he met four blank stares.

"Do you cherish the illusion," Ivor asked, "that he'll go into court and say so?"

"If he won't," said Edmund, "his companion will."

"Lord Wilversham, I'll bet," said Ivor. "Well, if you think you'll get *him* into the witness box to state that he saw you coming out of the flat of two peculiar old ladies with an ex-prisoner under the influence, then you're not showing the sense you've led us to expect you to show."

"Take it this way," said Jonathon. "They're your cousins and we all like them—but be honest: if they were strangers and they told you a tale of midnight and ginger wine, would you, would you take them seriously? You would not." He dropped into a brilliant caricature: " 'Officer, will you kindly take this *down*? Freddie dear, speak up. We make the wine ourselves, officer; it goes so well with the delicious curry my sister makes.' "

"You see that?" Ramon spread his hand expressively.

"It is true," Leonie said. "Nobody will believe what they say, and in our opinion—the four of us—it is too much risk for Teck. And perhaps even you, Mr. Forth, cannot know what we feel for Teck. He is a good man, and he has been so good, so very good to us all. The truth is good, but in this case we think that it is not good enough. We do not wish to see Teck going once again to prison. I cannot speak for the others, but I myself wish to help by saying that Teck was with me at that time. When they question me, I shall not give way as your cousins would give way. I am sorry, but I do not think you realise that we are trying to keep Teck out of prison."

"A quick way of sending him there," said Edmund, "is for the four of you to stand up in court and try to prove that he was in four places at once. Can't you use your heads? And haven't any of you ever heard of a little thing called perjury?"

"The truth, in this case, won't do," Jonathon pointed out. "They'll run rings round poor old Louisa and Frederica and have them admitting in the end that they were really out in China when the whole thing took place. You yourself will be telling the whole truth and nothing but the truth—but it won't sound at all convincing. You'll merely sound like a decent guy trying to back up his two demented cousins."

"Whereas the four of us," went on Ivor, "will at least make the judge scratch his head and try to find out which of us is lying. Swearing to tell nothing but the truth is all right, but lying in a good cause is better—and we're all agreed that Teck is a good cause. It's no use, Edmund; we're sticking to what we said."

"No, you're not." Edmund's voice was calm but firm. "You're not acting in a comic opera; you're going into a court of law. If you feel that the truth isn't going to weigh sufficiently as it stands, you can all pool your—"

He was brought to a stop by a yell of delight from Jonathon.

"He's got it! Edmund, you're a wonder!" He was thumping Edmund enthusiastically on the shoulder. "Of *course* that's the solution! We simply pool our evidence. We—"

"Please?" begged Ramon.

"United we stand, divided we make ruddy fools of ourselves," explained Ivor. "Edmund's got the answer. We don't trail red herrings; we merely underwrite what Edmund and his cousins say. We make the truth stick. If the prosecution's got a leg to stand on after we're through, I'll eat the judge's wig. We— Look, Ramon, will you take that wild ass look off your face and come and sit down. Come on, Leonie. Come on, you others. We're going to sit down here now and work this thing out. Ready?"

They sat down, and under Jonathon's instructions, worked it out.

241

Chapter Thirteen

Edmund, driving home, tried to imagine what effect trouble was having on Fran. He had seen her angry, he had seen her tearful, but he had never seen her really depressed.

Whatever he imagined was short of the astonishing truth: the events of the past few days had done what he had believed could never be done; they had reduced her to silence.

She was weeping on the sofa when he entered. Welty and Euphonia, following cautiously on his heels, intimated by signs and wildly rolling eyes that they had done their best to stem the flow, and had not succeeded. Putting them out and closing the door, Edmund applied himself to the task, but had only slightly more success; she transferred her head from the sofa arm to his chest, and went on weeping. After one or two attempts to reason, to soothe, he was silent, holding her in his arms until the flood had subsided. Then he shook out his large handkerchief, wiped her face and spoke calmly. "Now," he said. "Talk."

"There's n-nothing to say."

"There's plenty to say, and I'm used to hearing you say

it."

"There's nothing to say. Look what you've been dragged into!"

"Nobody," he said, "has done any dragging. I shall give evidence, Teck will be cleared and the whole thing will be forgotten. You're not, I hope, in favour of keeping Louisa and Frederica out of this?"

"No. The truth is the truth. And I knew—"

"You knew what?"

"I knew Teck was keeping something back. When they'd gone to the police, he admitted that he remembered going to their flat—but he couldn't say so, for fear of—of—"

"Dragging them in?"

"Yes."

"Don't get this out of focus," he said. "The Forths are nobody in particular, and never have been. They—"

"You don't have to be anybody in particular to want to keep out of the cheap headlines."

"True—but my uncle's motives for trying to keep out are even cheaper than that."

"He's trying to get into Parliament, and this might spoil it. Would you like that, if it were you?"

"Probably not. But coming forward to confirm that an accused man couldn't have been where he was when they said he was—is that likely to blast anybody's future?"

"Yes, if there are things about the case that will make him

look ridiculous. Jonathon and Leonie and the others won't take back what they said, and everything that Louisa and Frederica say—"

"Jonathon and Leonie and the others are going to retract their statements. They—"

"Retract? Take them back?"

"Just so. Their evidence is going to be of the supporting and not the undermining kind."

"Well, whichever"—her tone was lifeless—"this is going to be the end of Kerry and Belinda's schools. They've swallowed enough."

"Aren't there other schools?"

"Yes. Non-public. That's where I should have sent them in the first place, but I was afraid. I never had any illusions about our background, but it takes courage to turn your back on what you've imagined to be your right sphere—the best schools and all that goes with them. I didn't have that kind of courage. But when this is all over, I'm going to sell the house and—"

"Why sell the house?"

"Because nobody can stay in it after the kind of publicity Angela Wilde told me we're going to get."

There was a brief, tense silence.

"What did Angela Wilde tell you?" he asked.

"This." She fumbled in her bag, took out a letter and handed it to him.

It was short, and very much to the point. It merely outlined what Angela had told him; her reasons for writing, she stated, were to make clear certain things which he himself might not feel able to mention. Both the writer and the reader, it ended, liked him too much, had his interests too much at heart, to want to risk making him a laughing stock, and she was hers sincerely.

He sat holding the letter for a long time without speaking. If he had shown any sign, in the office earlier today, of changing sides once more, she would have made things easier for him, would have clinched the matter by telling him that she had already relieved him of the necessity of explaining anything to his friends...friend...at Campden Heights.

The letter, he thought, was unimportant. What was important was the fact that he had known the writer for months and had persuaded himself that she would make him a desirable wife. What was important was the fact that, but for meeting Fran Nash, no searchlight would ever have shone on his way of life, lighting it up in all its hollowness.

He tore the letter slowly into pieces and, making a ball of them, threw it into the fire.

"That doesn't change anything," Fran said. "I'm not going to marry you, Edmund."

"No? Why?" he asked, in a matter-of-fact tone.

"Because I love you, that's why. From the moment you met me, things have gone wrong for you."

"From the moment I met you, things have...Don't you understand that this is the first time in my life I've been really, *consciously,* continuously happy? I wake up happy, and I go to bed happy, and in between, I'm happy thinking about you, seeing you, being near you. I imagined, before I met you, that happiness was a negative state. You've taught me that it isn't."

She spoke steadily.

"I don't want to marry you," she said. "At any rate, not yet. I love you very much, but I don't think it's right to marry you and saddle you with two children and an old man who's been in prison. I think the most sensible thing I can do is sell up at Campden Heights and get out of London and live somewhere up North, where it's cheaper, in a place where Kerry and Belinda can go to day schools."

"You've really thought it all out?"

"Yes."

"You must do," he said gravely, "anything you think best."

She looked at him and he saw the tears start to her eyes. "Aren't you even going to t-talk about it?"

"No," he said. "At this moment, I'm not."

"Aren't you even going to p-persuade me?"

"No. You can only reason with people when they're in a reasonable mood, and at present you're not. I'm going to take you home and leave you there, and from now until the trial, I'm not going to see you, because I think that's wise. When Kerry and Belinda's schools break up, I shall take them—

with your permission—up to Mrs. Hugh Sefton, who'll be delighted to have them. If you're tackled by reporters, just say 'No comment' and go on saying it—and tell the others to do the same. The one thing you've got to avoid is giving facts of any kind—facts about yourself, about Teck, about the boarders. They won't get anything out of Jonathon; he's all right. So's Ivor. Leonie's discreet and Ramon doesn't talk enough English to do any harm. Don't go out more than you have to. And when it's all over, we shall discuss unessentials like marriage. Any questions?"

"No. Yes. Do you really love me?"

"With all my heart. Anything else?"

She laid his hand against her cheek.

"Nothing that matters," she said.

The Court proceedings drew a large and diverse crowd. As it grew larger, it became clear that not everybody would be able to find room inside, and it became necessary to establish priorities. A series of short but sharp struggles ensued, in the first of which Messrs. Ernest Derry and Sons, fruit and vegetable merchants, accustomed to handling heavy loads, disposed without difficulty of the dozen or so waiters from the Rimbault Restaurant.

Thereafter, they met with more determined opposition. The Spanish dancers, having come without more orthodox weapons, resorted to teeth tactics which Mr. Derry and his sons considered unsportsmanlike in the extreme. They were reinforced, moreover, by the entire cast of the play 'Apples of Gold', and after a brief, bloody battle, Mr. Derry awarded them second place in the queue.

Mr. Sefton, using his umbrella to great effect, fought his way to a good position, only to be met and defeated by four battered and dishevelled individuals who were being urged on by croaking battle cries from the aged but still formidable Countess of Dellston. Miss Brady was rescued from the mêlée by two junior members of the office staff and taken home in a taxi.

By the time police reinforcements had been rushed to the scene, Mr. Derry had marshalled the victors into an orderly line. Mr. Sefton went home, tended his wounds and sat down to wait for the evening papers.

From these, he and several million others learned that the proceedings in court had been far from dull. Those who had fought for admission, all being strongly partisan, had given noisy demonstrations of their sympathies, and there had been more than one threat to clear the court.

Mr. Jonathon Dee's evidence was reported by the papers in full. Under cross-examination, he said that he remembered having been shown a bracelet by the plaintiff, but in his opinion it was entirely valueless, not to say Christmas- cracker-ish, and the plaintiff was mistaken in supposing it to be worth anything. Questioned further, he intimated that the plaintiff had entirely mistaken his feelings for her; they were far from warm. He said that he was not aware that the bracelet was an heirloom; the plaintiff had informed him that it had been given to her by an Italian prince; this was no doubt another mistake. The witness managed to convey the impression that in describing herself as an actress, the plaintiff had made the greatest mistake of all.

Miss Louisa Forth's evidence was given forcefully, and she was several times asked by the judge to keep to the point. Her sister's barely-audible testimony was difficult to follow, in spite of repeated urgings from the gallery to "Speak Up, Freddie."

Mr. Edmund Forth's evidence was given quietly and clearly. Thereafter there was little quiet, as the subsequent proceedings were enlivened by repeated offers from the waiters of the Rimbault Restaurant and the entire company of Sevillanas to take the stand and vindicate the accused.

Mr. Ivor Breck said that on the opening night of the play "Apples of Gold" he had been invited by Mademoiselle Rimbault to sup at the Rimbault Restaurant in Century Street. As he left the theatre, he met the accused and invited him to accompany him. They proceeded to Century Street and on the way met the company of dancers known as the Sevillanas, who had hurried from the Frank Eddleston Hall in Brixton at the conclusion of their own performance in the hope of seeing something of Mr. Jonathon Dee's. Hearing that they were too late, they decided to accompany Mr. Breck and the accused to the Rimbault Restaurant. On their arrival, they were welcomed by Mademoiselle Rimbault, but the accused refused her offer of supper and said that he was going to pay a short visit to the flat of Miss Louisa Forth. He waited only to drink a toast to the success of the play, and then the entire party—Mademoiselle Rimbault, Mr. Breck, the company of Sevillanas and the waiters from the restaurant —decided to accompany the accused to Miss Forth's. They went with him, waited to see him admitted, and then dispersed. The time was a quarter to twelve.

This testimony was supported in the witness box by Mademoiselle Rimbault and the dancer known as Ramon, and by the vast majority of spectators from the body of the court.

Order having been restored, Mr. Van Willans was called.

He answered questions unwillingly, and with increasing brusqueness. Asked why he lived under an assumed name, he said that it was because he was sick and tired of being pestered by reporters who pressed for interviews in order to find out how he felt about living in straitened circumstances while his pictures made fortunes for others. He was only too glad, he stated, that people who had bought his work despite unfavourable notices from critics were now being rewarded for their clear-sightedness. His early works, which had been considered almost beneath critical notice, were now in the five figure bracket, where they deserved to be. It was a pity that so many had been allowed to go out of the country, but it was satisfying to know that the majority were hanging in the homes of private collectors.

Asked to keep to the matter in hand, Mr. van Willans said that if the case proved anything at all, it was the old proverb about giving a dog a bad name. Here was a man being tried not because anybody believed for a moment that he would take a trumpery bracelet, but because he was considered a good subject for suspicion. If a man tried to start afresh, nobody would allow him to. Here was he himself doing his best to live in decent obscurity, only to be dragged out and asked impertinent questions. Publicity was the plague of modern living and it was all right for those who liked it and enjoyed nothing so much as cutting capers in the limelight, but there were limits and this was going beyond them.

Asked once more to keep to the point, Mr. van Willans said that he had not wanted to get into the witness box in the first place, and was only too willing to get out of it if asked. Questioned as to his movements on the opening night of the play, he stated that he had left the theatre and gone to visit a sick man to give him an account of it. He had told him that it was not worth going to see except for Mr. Jonathon Dee's performance, which was of exceptional merit and great promise. He had then gone home and said a civil word to Mr. Edmund Forth when he brought Teck home, and that was all, and anybody could quote him with regard to the play, even if it wasn't in line with what the critics had said about it. Critics, pah! If anybody was interested, the picture found recently in a junk shop and said by critics and experts— experts, bah!—to be his work, was not his work at all.

The sensation caused by this disclosure was long in dying down. No further witnesses were called, and proceedings were brought to a close with as much speed as possible. The accused was acquitted and carried shoulder high from the court, while the judge made plans to go into the country for rest and recuperation.

Edmund went immediately to Mr. Sefton's flat.

"Well, that's that, and no bones broken," said Mr. Sefton. "A drink?"

"Several strong ones," said Edmund. "George, I want your help."

"Well?"

"I'm taking Louisa and Frederica away."

Mr. Sefton came back from the sideboard, drinks in hand.

"Here; get that down you," he said. "Where are you taking Louisa and Frederica to, and when are you taking them?"

Edmund drained his glass and gave a sigh of pleasure.

"Tonight. I told them to pack and I told them to say nothing to anybody. If I don't get them away, there'll be a horde of reporters in the street tomorrow trying to get stories. I'm taking them to Montebarca."

"Are you going to leave them there?"

"For the present. If they decide to stay permanently, they can. They like the place, and they'll be happy there—and well looked after for the rest of their lives."

"Which," said Mr. Sefton thoughtfully, "is a point. Looking after the ageing or the infirm is a problem in this country, as somebody's going to find out when I'm a bit older. So long as people keep fit, they're all right on their own; it's when age catches up on them that the trouble begins. Funny thing: I always had an idea you might settle out there. Are you going to?"

"It depends."

"I see. Well, what's this help you want from me?"

"I want to be kept in touch."

"With Fran?"

"Yes. Will you keep an eye on her?"

"It'll be a pleasure."

"And report to me."

"I will. Why don't you take her too?"

"Just at this moment, she wouldn't come. She's tired and she's been through a lot and I'm not going to press her too far. Not yet. I'm off, George. Look after the office. And look after Fran."

Welty and Euphonia helped him to load the car. Then, with Louisa and Frederica tucked comfortably into the back, he took the road to the coast.

The drive began in snow and ended in rain. Portugal was awash, but it was green and glistening. As they sighted the Roman aqueduct at Elvas, memory stirred and woke in the two old ladies; by the time they reached Montebarca, the past had come back in force.

Their arrival proved to Edmund, if he had not known it already, that the Portuguese peasant memory was long, and in

253

this case, loving. He need have no fear that Louisa and Frederica would ever lack affectionate care or attention.

The water colours were in place, and nobody gave him
away.

They were at Montebarca for two weeks before a letter
came from Mr. Sefton. Edmund read it, and then drove into
Elvas and sent his godfather a long and detailed telegram.

A few days later, Mr. Sefton picked up Jonathon Dee at his
new flat and drove with him to Number 11 Campden Heights.
A line of cars stood outside the building.

"You're absolutely certain Fran'll be here?" Mr. Sefton
asked.

"Positive," Jonathon answered. "She told me she wanted
to see how things went."

"Then let's go in. The others?"

"Ramon, as I told you, is in Paris with the company. They
come back to London in June—to a real theatre. Did I remember to tell you that the Rimbault's packed every lunch and dinner time?"

"Yes. And you're playing to packed houses. I gather you're
the big draw—but you've got a pretty level head, and I daresay
you'll keep it. Heard from Ivor?"

"Yes. The old girl's made most of the money over to him
—but he's got to stay up in Yorkshire until she dies."

Mr Sefton was craning his neck to see over the heads of
the people assembled in the hall.

"Can't see Fran," he said.

"Over there, by the stairs," said Jonathon. "Hasn't she written to Edmund at all?"

"No. Wouldn't even answer his letters. Maybe this idea of his will do the trick. They're beginning, aren't they? You'd better take your side and I'll take mine. Where's Leonie?"

"Over there. Did you brief her?"

"Yes. Here we go."

They separated, and the sale of furniture began. The first few items in the hall went for almost nothing, and the auctioneer moved to the drawing-room and clambered with his clerk on to an improvised dais. Jonathon went to the corner by the piano; Mr. Sefton stood by the bookcase and Leonie took up a position in the middle of the room.

With the sale of the piano, the bidding suddenly began to show signs of looking up. To the evident astonishment of the auctioneer, the price, after sticking at five pounds, was taken by a foreign lady to ten. A young man, easily recognisable as Jonathon Dee, the newly-famous actor, made a bid of fifteen, and an old gentleman standing by the bookcase took the price to twenty.

"Twenty pounds," said the reviving auctioneer. "Am I offered any advance on—Thank you, Madam. Forty, Fifty. Fifty from the— Sixty. Sixty pounds for this—thank you, sir. Seventy. Eighty, Eighty pounds to the gentleman in the corner. One hundred; thank you, Madam. Two hundred, Three. I am

offered," shouted the auctioneer, galvanised, "three hundred—
Four. I am—thank you, Madam. Six. Any advance on— Seven. Seven hundred pounds. Any advance on seven hundred
pounds? Going, going"—the hammer crashed—"gone. Sold
to the gentleman in the corner. Lot Number eighteen: this"—
the auctioneer looked at it with well-simulated pride—"this
charming little mahogany table. What am I bid for this?—Ten
pounds. Thank you, Madam. Twenty. Thirty. Any advance
on—Thank you sir. Forty ..."

Fran, tight-lipped, made her way through the press and
halted beside Mr. Sefton.

"Stop it!" she hissed. "Stop it at once!"

Mr. Sefton, looking over her head at the auctioneer, sent
the price of the sofa rocketing.

"Stop it —*please!*" begged Fran. "People are beginning
to—"

"Sold," chanted the auctioneer, "to the gentleman in the
corner. Lot Number—"

"What are you doing? Oh, what are you doing?" moaned
Fran.

"I'm buying under instructions from a client of mine in
Portugal," said Mr. Sefton.

"The things are worth nothing, and you know it."

"The things," said Mr. Sefton, signalling to the auctioneer, "have a certain sentimental value for my client. He plans
to use them for furnishing a small house for two old ladies.

The place was once occupied by an employee on my client's estate, but the man is marrying and moving out, so the two old ladies will soon be moving in."

"Sold," carolled the auctioneer, "to the gentleman in the corner."

"Please, *please* don't throw away any more money. Please! The things are rubbishy, and you know it."

"They'll go awfully well," said Mr. Sefton, "with Swati rugs and Benares pottery."

"Sold," sang the auctioneer, "to the gentleman in the corner."

"Are you going to stop this tomfoolery, or are you not?" demanded Fran.

"I am acting under specific instructions received by telegram from Elvas," said Mr. Sefton. "Any objections you have must be addressed, I'm afraid, to my client. He is—"

He stopped. Fran had turned on her heel and walked through the crowd and out of the room. She had said nothing, but Mr. Sefton, looking across the room at Leonie and Jonathon, smiled with the utmost satisfaction and raised both his thumbs in a gesture of triumph.

Chapter Fourteen

"And there," said Louisa, "is where we plan to put our little Kashmiri cake stand. And the rugs there, and Freddie's pictures...Edmund, are you *sure* you won't mind parting with her pictures?"

"I would like to see them hanging on these walls," he said with perfect truth.

"We're so grateful to you, dear boy. Whoever would have dreamed," she asked, following Frederica out into the sunshine and waiting for Edmund to join them, "whoever would have dreamed of imagining Freddie and myself here in a dear little house of our own at Montebarca. How happy Walter would have been if he had known!"

They walked slowly back to the main house and went inside. Edmund was on his way to his own room when Louisa stopped him.

"Edmund dear, could you spare a moment? Freddie and I have something rather important to say to you."

He followed them into the drawing-room and sat facing the two of them. They gazed at him solemnly.

"We have decided, Edmund," began Louisa, "to touch on a matter which we feel is one upon which you will allow us to offer you a little advice. A little womanly advice."

He waited.

"Before the dreadful business of the bracelet," went on Louisa, "Freddie and I were so happy to see how well things were going between you and dear, dear Fran. May I go on ?"

"Please do."

"You most kindly brought us out here; you have most kindly settled us here. When our little bits and pieces arrive, all we shall have to do is arrange them in our own little house. But you...will you forgive us both for seeming to intrude? — you have shown no sign of wanting to go back to England. Freddie and I are anxious to make you understand that you need not stay here on our account. We are only too anxious, strange though this may sound, to see you leave. Pretty girls, dear boy do not grow on trees—not girls as pretty and as good as Fran. You cannot leave them too long. You have been with us for nearly four weeks, and Freddie and I feel most strongly that you should—that you should—"

"Go to her," piped Freddie with unusual resolution.

Edmund had risen and was standing at the window, his eyes on the quiet, lovely scene.

"And so," said Louisa, to his profile, "we hope very much that—" She paused. "Did you hear anything?"

"Yes," said Edmund. "You were saying?"

It might be a trick of the imagination. He had heard it, sleeping and waking, since his arrival at Montebarca. He had heard it...

And then, his heart beating suffocatingly, he saw what he had been waiting for for so long.

Through his daze of relief and happiness, he found one part of his mind making cool, detached calculations. If she tried to take that bend at that pace, she would... Yes. One would think that road would have been wide enough for six large black cars. Stuck. Well and truly stuck. Those two children had grown since he first saw them stranded on the roadside. Look at them now: almost up to Teck's white temples.

Wait for it. Oh, wait for it. What was Louisa saying?

"And so you must go, dear boy. You must go to her. You must—"

She paused, her head held on one side in a listening attitude.

"There it is again," he said. "Did you hear it, Edmund? Wasn't that a—"

He answered as he went swiftly out of the room, out of the house.

"It was a whistle," he said.

THE END

The Fox From His Lair

by

Elizabeth Cadell

It couldn't be. He was thousands of miles away, and everybody had said, with conviction, that he would never come back. It was a resemblance, that was all; this was Portugal, and on every side were men with dark hair and dark eyes and ...

But there was no mistaking that expression : a mixture of the bland and the sardonic. There was no mistaking that lean figure or even that too-familiar attitude. It couldn't, it couldn't be ...

She ventured one more glance. It was.

The airport, the laughing, breathless boys, the scattered figures on the tarmac and behind the railing, all disappeared. For moments, she was back in the garden of her home, shouting with hatred at the enemy leaning negligently over the wall—the enemy who had ruined every holiday and every outdoor project, who had throughout the long years of her childhood defeated, effortlessly, every attempt at revenge.

Angus Pemberton.

The past receded. She was back in the Lisbon sunshine, playing with her two nephews. She could only hope that Angus Pemberton was not on his way home—but it was hardly possible, she remembered with relief; he had been thrown out by his grandmother, who had stated positively that he had gone for good—for everybody's good.

There was a hope that he had not recognised her. It was, she calculated, seven years since he had left Steyne. She had been eighteen, and although she could not have changed in essentials, fashions made an effective disguise; he might trace a likeness, but that would be all.

The hope weakened when she saw, without seeming to see, that he had left the balcony. It revived for a moment as he hesitated outside the airport buildings—and died when he began a leisurely, long-legged, purposeful approach.

There was no chance of moving away, even if she had wanted to; the boys had caught her during her moment off-guard, and she was encircled by their arms. She glanced at her watch: twenty minutes before the plane was due to leave; Mrs. Jansen, anxious to avoid a last luncheon, had stated that they must be at the airport in good time—and so they had been.

She could hear, behind her, the firm footsteps. Then the slow, deep voice—that, too, she remembered well.

"Aren't you...surely you're Anabelle Baird?"

She turned. She managed a smile, but her greeting was cool.

"Hello, Angus. What are you doing here?"

"Waiting for a hired car. I ordered one, but it wasn't here when I flew in. It's on its way. And you?"

"I'm going up to Oporto."

"You married"—his eyes went to the boys—"a Portuguese?"

"These are Clare's children."

He smiled. Well might he smile, she reflected bitterly; it had taken him ten minutes and a lift of the eyebrows to transform Clare's lifelong enmity into a river of devotion that had almost, but unfortunately not quite, drowned him.

He was screwing up his eyes in calculation.

"Clare was, let me see, seventeen when I left. And pretty. Did she marry that concert pianist?"

"No."

"The architect—what was his name?"

"No."

"The fellow with the woolly hair, who called me a low swine?"

"No. She married Keith Trevor, a journalist."

"Lucky journalist. What are you doing with her children?"

"I'm looking after them."

"And doing it remarkably well."

There it was—that sardonic note she knew so well.

"Didn't you marry anybody?" he asked.

He hadn't, she noticed—and it did not increase her regard for him—made any pretence of listing the candidates. She had to face it; she had, in fact, faced it long ago; she wasn't the type that made men catch fire.

"No, I didn't marry anybody," she said.

There was a pause while he studied her frankly—to assess, she thought, exactly where she had missed out. She felt the colour rising to her cheeks, but she met his gaze steadily.

∞

End of preview.

To continue reading, look for the book entitled: "The Fox From His Lair" by Elizabeth Cadell

About the Author

Elizabeth Vandyke was born in British India at the beginning of the 20th century. She married a young Scotsman and became Elizabeth Cadell, remaining in India until the illness and death of her much-loved husband found her in England, with a son and a daughter to bring up, at the beginning of World War 2. At the end of the war she published her first book, a light-hearted depiction of the family life she loved. Humour and optimism conquered sorrow and widowhood, and the many books she wrote won her a wide public, besides enabling her to educate her children (her son joined the British Navy and became an Admiral), and allowing her to travel, which she loved. Spain, France and Portugal provide a background to many of her books, although England and India were not forgotten. She finally settled in Portugal, where her married daughter still lives, and died when well into her 80s, much missed by her 7 grandchildren, who had all benefitted from her humour, wisdom and gentle teaching. British India is now only a memory, and the quiet English village life that Elizabeth Cadell wrote about has changed a great deal, but her vivid characters, their love affairs and the tears and laughter they provoke, still attract many readers, young and not-so-young, in this twenty-first century. Reprinting these books will please her fans and it is hoped will win her new ones.

Also by Elizabeth Cadell

My Dear Aunt Flora
Fishy, Said the Admiral
River Lodge
Family Gathering
Iris in Winter
Sun in the Morning
The Greenwood Shady
The Frenchman & the Lady
Men & Angels
Journey's Eve
Spring Green
The Gentlemen Go By
The Cuckoo in Spring
Money to Burn
The Lark Shall Sing
Consider The Lilies
The Blue Sky of Spring
Bridal Array
Shadow on the Water
Sugar Candy Cottage
The Green Empress
Alice Where Art Thou?
The Yellow Brick Road
Six Impossible Things
Honey For Tea
The Language of the Heart
Mixed Marriage

Letter to My Love
Death Among Friends
Be My Guest
Canary Yellow
The Fox From His Lair
The Corner Shop
The Stratton Story
The Golden Collar
The Past Tense of Love
The Friendly Air
Home for the Wedding
The Haymaker
Deck With Flowers
The Fledgling
Game in Diamonds
Parson's House
Round Dozen
Return Match
The Marrying Kind
Any Two Can Play
A Lion in the Way
Remains to be Seen
The Waiting Game
The Empty Nest
Out of the Rain
Death and Miss Dane

Afterword

Note: Elizabeth Cadell is a British author who wrote her books using the traditional British spelling. Therefore because these books are being published worldwide, the heirs have agreed to keep her books exactly as she wrote them and not change the spelling.

Made in the USA
Middletown, DE
12 December 2021

55382080R00156